Federation

P.G. Redstone

The Journey Begins.

Cover design: Jonathan Stien
Illustrations: Nicole Pouilloux
ISBN#: 978-0-9673590-1-4
ROJée Crumbe Films, Inc.
P.O. Box 62034, Littleton, Colorado 80162

With special thanks to Jonathan Stien and Dawn Nelson
for their immeasurable creative assistance.

he journey from Kamakura to Kyoto takes twelve days. If you travel for eleven but stop with only one day remaining, how can you admire the moon over the capital?

Nichiren Daishonin – Letter to Niike

$\mathcal{P}rologue$

THE MOON OVER THE MOUNTAIN

 *IN A SMALL BODY OF WATER* where silence and stars prevail, where underground hot springs send vapors to tiptoe over the water's silvery surface – the only clouds in the clear night air – there swims a woman. Lithe and sensual, she swims naked and alone, except for the mountains that surround her. The woman has a name, but tonight she has forgotten it. In another life, in another dimension, perhaps her name was Katie. Here, where the moon blankets reality in pure velvet, names have no bearing. No relevance. Nothing matters. Nothing echoes. Nothing makes a sound.

The woman who might be Katie treads water, staring at the moon in quiet expectation. Then, as if to grant her unspoken wish, another moon appears from behind a neighboring mountain peak.

As the two moons shine brightly over her planet, tears fill the young woman's eyes, and she cries for all of those who have come before her – those who, armed with nothing more than their own humanity, have made the world a kinder, sweeter place to live.

Muriel

THE LEGACY

SHE HAD NEVER BEEN ALLOWED to hold him. That had been part of the etiquette, the way-it-must-be of it, and she'd been good to her promise. She'd had a chance to see his face though, the roundness of him, the jerking and shaking of his tiny limbs, the outstretched fingers that trembled at the emptiness around them. And she'd managed not to cry when they had taken him away, leaving only a silent nurse to bathe her vitals with soap and warm water as if to erase the whole of her pain.

It was only a few years after the end of the Second World War, and not a hospitable time for a woman in Muriel's predicament. Young and innocent except for that one night of passion, she was well into her pregnancy before she fully understood what was happening to her body. Her periods had abruptly ended, zipping her skirts had become an ordeal, and the nausea that held her in its grip was unrelenting. And it wasn't until the friend with whom she shared a room at the boarding house sat her down and made her stare unblinkingly at the facts in front of her that she admitted to herself in a flood of tears that she was really pregnant.

She would never see the father of her child again after that one night together. They'd made love under a chestnut tree – the most beautiful place on Earth, Muriel had reflected as she'd watched the stars dance through the branches. Hours later she'd gone back to her room and her reputation, and he'd disappeared into the night, frightened away by the power of her emotions, as well as his own, vaguely aware that he'd made contact with a fallen angel. A boy of seventeen, Muriel had been a conquest for him, an adventure, a story to be told to friends who could keep a secret. And those who could not. But, for Muriel, in whose womb his seed would germinate, the night would not end so quickly.

She'd chosen to have the baby because it was the only choice that made sense at such a late point in her pregnancy. But also because, now that she recognized the fluttering in her stomach as the flip-flops of her unborn child, the baby had quickly taken on an identity of its own. *It* was apparently meant to be.

Her friend had suggested inventing some sort of back story that would placate their neighbors and co-workers. An absentee husband perhaps – one who would soon be joining her. But, in the end, Muriel had simply put up with the whispers and sneering, and bravely gone ahead with the whole thing, doing her best to ignore those who took pleasure in disapproving.

Giving the baby up for adoption was especially difficult for Muriel, as she was the most natural of mothers and found it difficult to disenfranchise herself from what would turn out to be the only child she would ever carry. But the adoptive parents were warm and kind and solid, making it easier for Muriel to hand over her prize. Still, for the rest of her days, Muriel was unable to hear a baby's cry without thinking of her own child, without hearing him wail and then whimper at the shock of his advent into the world.

Muriel had never set out in life to achieve greatness. Raised on a farm, she'd milked cows, cleaned stables, and poached eggs to perfection. She'd done it without complaint and with a steady hand on the reins of her imagination, which bucked and heaved with dreams of a world beyond the barn door. At a moment of readiness, with nothing more than a suitcase, a small wad of bills, and a tube of red lipstick, she set out in the world in pursuit of her budding, but undefined ambitions. And, in spite of the poignant interlude – love found, love lost, child given, child taken away – or maybe because of it – she quickly found her purpose.

As a young woman, there was little about Muriel's physical self that foreshadowed the beauty of her later years. Tall and gawky and painfully shy, she lacked the confidence that would one day bring new definition to her features. Still, her eyes were so blue and so utterly captivating that even people walking by her on the street got lost in them. And with time, the depth and beauty of her eyes would come to be matched by the rest of her, and she would take on an aura that even her enemies would have to concede was dazzling. Once a milkmaid, she became a goddess who tripped over her own two feet and made you think the dance divine.

She met Samuel Cagle somewhere down the road to divinity, gracing him with a passing smile that he largely ignored in favor of counting his own footsteps. Not a physically attractive man, he seemed to expend the bulk of his energy nursing a troubled mind, a thing which greatly peaked Muriel's interest – and to exude a painful neediness, which further excited her maternal instincts. As the founder of the Movement for the Federation of Earth, Samuel made room for little in his life beyond this all-consuming cause. Maybe it was because Muriel saw in him the greatest challenge of her life; maybe it was because the cause he held dear fascinated her like no other – whatever the case, she made up her mind not just to win him, but to spend the rest of her life with him. She told herself that love was something she would willingly live without (after all, it had only brought her pain so far). But to share a partnership, to share a mission in life, now that would be something extraordinary!

As a pacifist and self-appointed goodwill ambassador on behalf of the Movement for the Federation of Earth, Muriel would travel the world, meeting with various leaders, dignitaries and intellectuals, most of whom walked away from the experience with greater empathy for a subject that had been, up until then, unwelcome – if not downright taboo.

At Muriel's insistence, she and Samuel had given up the idea of having children of their own. There were so many needy children, she had argued with surprising success, never sharing with him the loss of her only child. In truth, Samuel was ambivalent about the whole subject and only went along with her, as he often did, simply because it was the expedient thing to do. And so they had eventually found their little girl, five-year-old Katie, born in France, whose parents – an Indian father and Algerian mother – had been killed on impact by a drunk driver while Katie slept peacefully on the floor of their vehicle. Muriel had flown to France to meet the child, and it had been love at first sight for both of them. They had fallen into each other's arms and hugged and cried as if reunited after an absence that spanned many lifetimes. And this closeness between them, this indivisibility, would remain strong for the rest of Muriel's life.

But Muriel's life would not be an easy one, both because she had married into complexity and because she welcomed with open arms the challenges of a world in crisis. As those who knew her understood, Muriel was the passion behind Samuel's intellect, the patience fueling the endless task, the force of love that would spawn a new generation of true-believers.

And her seeds, along with the seeds of other like-minded activists, would bear fruit. The world would survive its many crises and, as Muriel had so often anticipated in her unflagging dreams of a better world, would eventually come together as One.

But, by the year 2030, the official Year of Federation, Muriel Cagle was no longer a tangible part of life on Earth. The dream she had fostered and nurtured for more than half a century had found its way to fruition – taking on new dimensions in the process – a tiny rivulet that finds its way through the impasses, first this way, then that, growing proportionately with the downpour and with the size of merging rivulets along the way, becoming at last an unstoppable river.

Barcelona

FEDERATION DAY
JULY 17, 2030

———

 *A WORLD WITHOUT BOUNDARIES,* he mused, as he handed over his American e-passport for what he figured would probably be the last time and stood in place for the biometric eye scan. A citizen of the world. He liked the sound of that.

The customs official waved him through now with a respectful, almost apologetic, smile. As Secretary of State, he'd always been able to rely on the protocol of diplomatic immunity to speed him through customs, conveniently avoiding the random inspections that used to drive him crazy as an everyday citizen. How long had it been, he asked himself, since he'd been detained just for the look in his eye and the length of his hair?

Tall and handsome, with the sandy-gray hair of a mid-life blonde, there was something in RJ's eyes that radiated an inner gentility. Still, there was an emptiness there that surfaced in moments alone with his thoughts which – as he edged his way through the terminal doors that would reunite him with Barcelona – were at his fiftieth birthday. *Fifty! How the hell did it happen, anyway? One day a boy on the verge of manhood, the next*

–

And then it hit him – the air from the open door, soft on his face, up his nostrils, through his hair. How could the air still be the same and he be so different? *Fifty!* Well, fifty-six actually. And still counting. Obsessively perhaps.

But now with the sun on his face and the noise from the streets, and the language that rolled off everyone's tongue but his own, the obsession ended, eclipsed by the physical thrill of simply being alive. Ushered into the waiting limo, he went reluctantly, an acquiescent prisoner.

God, he loved the sweet, soft fragrance of the air!

"How long has it been?" he heard his aide ask.

"Thirty-three years." The answer spilled off his lips as if waiting at the edge of his mouth for the opportunity. *Barcelona!* Why *had* it taken him so long to return? The question lingered.

They passed the monument to Christopher Columbus – the one that pigeons liked to think of as their own – and RJ touched a fingertip to the scar that ran down his forehead and through his right eyebrow. It was a habit he'd developed over the years – touching the wound in thought. No doubt somewhere along the way it had become the vehicle for getting in touch with himself, with the part of him eternally bound to the scar tissue.

He rolled down the window and let the air in. It was starting to cloud up now, but the air still felt good on his cheek, and he quickly faded into semi-sleep and half-dreams of nothing.

"Mr. Cutter! RJ! Sir!" The words were quiet but intense.

Opening his eyes, RJ smiled briefly at his human alarm clock, noting with some dismay that the rain had started coming down.

"Federation Hall, Sir. On your left."

And there it was. Big as life. He'd been eager to see it in person, almost as eager as he'd been to see Barcelona again. As the limousine pulled past the gathering crowds, slowly making its way toward the imposing convention center that bore the flags of the nations of Earth, RJ conducted an internal self-quiz. Austria. Paraguay. France. Liberia. Sri Lanka. *They're getting tougher.* Kyrgyzstan. *Can't stump him.* The U.S. of A. Not the last one to ratify, but the one that made the biggest difference. The one nobody thought would ever take the step. *The deal-maker.*

"Just goes to show you ..." He said the words out loud.

"To show you what, Sir?"

And then he saw it, flying high above the others – simple, straightforward, waving boldly in the wind and rain as if to demonstrate its resilience, encompassing – no, transcending – the nations of Earth. A young girl had drawn the prototype, won the worldwide contest – at nine years old, the creator of the official flag of the Federation of Earth.

RJ watched as his Secret Service agents got out of the limousine, and flashed on a favorite old movie that he couldn't quite name. His aide got out of the car now and popped open his umbrella, inviting RJ under its shelter. Stepping out of the limo and under the waiting umbrella, RJ was quickly surrounded by reporters.

An American reporter managed to get to him first. "Give us the inside story, Mr. Secretary. What finally turned it around?"

"You know what they say about an idea whose time has come," RJ answered, half of him still trying to dig up the name of that old movie, the other half of him lost in the awe of the moment.

His aide was trying to hurry him on now but, despite the unrelenting rain and the dizzying sea of umbrellas, RJ wasn't feeling in any rush.

"How do you like Barcelona, Mr. Cutter?" came the question from an eager reporter with a thick Spanish accent.

"El cielo es tan ozul como el Meditteraneo." *The sky is as blue as the Mediterranean...* "El mar y el cielo son uno. The sun and the sky are one, yes?" RJ laughed out loud at the irony, then turned to his aide in an aside. "I memorized those words for the occasion and what do I get for all my trouble? A fucking downpour."

"Got any words for the nay-sayers?" an American reporter asked.

"There's a lesson in there somewhere," he finished. Then he smiled at the reporter – a smile as big and as real as the moment – and said, "Well, I guess this isn't their day, is it?"

Urged on by his entourage, RJ moved ahead of the flock and up the steps of Federation Hall, not feeling the least bit invested in his body – a mere appendage hanging on by a sliver of soul. He touched a finger to his face and found the scar. The magic was delivered.

He went inside.

It wasn't the idea of getting older that bothered him. It was just the fact that the years were going by. This he thought as he walked into the gaudy and glorious edifice, crowned with a modern monstrosity of a chandelier that caught the sun's rays and sent a profusion of colors dancing throughout the main hall. That and the fact that, inevitably, she had gotten older too. She who lived frozen in time in his uncompromising memory. He hated his lackluster brain for not knowing how to age her, but there was no artist in his psyche, no knowing what to change, what to wear down. And anyway, it wasn't her age that troubled him but, again, the simple fact that time was slipping by.

Still, with the passing of time, there were things to be proud of. The "great achievement," for one thing. The fruit of his life's ambition. That it actually came to be was more than he could sometimes absorb, and even today – even now at the moment of glory and celebration – he had trouble believing that humanity had actually been willing to take the giant step that would forever change the structure of world politics. The step that, with any luck, would bring hope of lasting peace to the planet and a promise of guardianship for the environment as a whole.

In retrospect, he could see that it hadn't come about exactly the way they had planned it. Ultimately, the Federation had been the child of many seeds and not the product of a single, isolated ideology – nor had it been simply the legislative empowerment of the United Nations. Rather, it had been the gradual result of open-ended dialogue among the people and powers of the world in the context of a planet in crisis. Someone had once told him that a unified world would come about only as the result of global cataclysm and, while this had not proven to be exactly the case, a variety of environmental and political crises had been deemed in sum cataclysmic enough to warrant the union of powers. To his satisfaction, constitutional world government had been the popular choice, though even the path to a viable constitution had not been a straight line, as he had naively believed it would be. There had been many drafts and many contributions, and the final product bore little resemblance to the document he had initially embraced with every ounce of his young and unsuspecting soul. Still, the achievement couldn't be ignored. And he had been a soldier on the front lines of political change, an operative part of the Movement.

RJ walked the circular staircase of Federation Hall with a kind of irrational but not unpleasant trepidation, as if they led from the certainties of Earth to the mysteries of heaven. The stairs were cold under his feet – made of marble, he remembered. Imported – but from where? *Gotta be in shape to do the stairs,* he thought to himself, running his hand along the banister in an effort to feel the reality of it all under his fingers. A step for every country of the world. *How many was that anyway?* But he couldn't remember, and his mind drifted into thinking that he was in pretty good shape for fifty.

Okay, fifty-six. But what was age anyway, in the context of – well, in the context of *everything*? All that really mattered – the thing that mattered most – was to see her again. Then again, the idea of meeting her face to face, eye to eye, filled him with a terrible angst. He'd wanted to see her again, back in the early days – called a few times and only gotten a machine. He'd done his best, over the years, to follow the twists and turns of her life, and once even made a feeble, late-night attempt to contact her when she'd answered the phone and he'd finally heard her voice again. But, for reasons that were never clear to him, he'd hung up at the prospect of actual contact.

Why he had chosen to avoid her back then, and then to put her out of his mind completely, he still wasn't quite sure. Something to do with losing his footing and falling into the darkness of lost souls, only to find at the end of the tunnel, the light of youthful freedom. Armed with that freedom, coupled with a certain amount of personal charm and a post-graduate degree in political science, he found himself on the road to Washington, D.C., where drugs and alcohol awaited him like a super-charged welcoming committee.

Oh, he didn't get in *too* deep. Not really. Just deep enough to change his perspective on life. To erase the picture from his memory, if only for a little while. Remarkably, their paths had never intersected, and after a time, the silence between them grew so great that he eventually forgot the sound of her voice and occasionally questioned her very reality – a reality he might have easily confirmed had he chosen to get on his computer and search for her, or pointedly questioned those in the know. And yet, at some level, the depths of which he seldom explored, he longed more than anything to see her again.

"What do you think, Sir?" asked his aide, now breathlessly walking the stairs at his side.

RJ gave him a cryptic smile in response, secretly resenting the interruption of his thought process, and quickly going back to it. What would she think if she saw him again? The extra twenty pounds, the thinning hair, the perpetual antacids, and – no, that wasn't it at all. He was still good-looking, and he knew it. One of those guys who had managed to age with enviable distinction, and with his boyish charm intact. Or so they told him.

But never mind all that. It was the inside of him that was eating at him now. Who was he – *on the inside*? What was he made of? At fifty. Fifty-six.

Whatever it was, she would see it. She would know. And maybe that, in the end, was why he'd stayed away. And maybe why now, with this final achievement – the one they had only dreamed of back then – he felt ready to be seen, to be recognized, to renew the simple but extraordinary friendship that had never really died. *Before it was too late.*

And so he put aside the big fear and, in a single, simple moment, gave the picture in his memory the liberty to move on. To get up from that sacred place on the sand, shake off her sweater, and – letting the drunken laughter spill from her heart – stroll down the beach to pick up pebbles by the side of the ocean. And in giving her life, he knew she would remember. And in remembering, she would come to him.

The man who made *casual* a popular word at the White House wore a black suit and a purple tie for the occasion. Standing at the podium, he looked out at representatives from all over the world, and wondered how long he'd been standing there, and whether there were words in his brain, much less the breath in his lungs to utter them. How had he ever gotten up on stage? Had someone really called his name? That was his name, wasn't it – *Randolph Jeremiah Cutter?*

He started to speak, but found nothing emanating from his mouth, except for the beginnings of a nervous cough. It wasn't like him to be nervous. It was so unlike him, in fact, that he had difficulty putting a label on the sensation. He'd given a hundred speeches before. Loved every minute of it – loved the feeling it gave him when, unimpeded by interruptions and objections, his views hit the airwaves and echoed through a room. It wasn't a surge of power that he got out of the experience – not exactly – more a feeling of total freedom – the kind of freedom on behalf of which revolutions had been waged and poems passionately penned. Freedom of self-expression. The right to be heard by all.

And now the eyes of the world were on him, he who had been given the honor to represent what he still liked to think of as the greatest country in the world. Here it was his turn at the podium, at this, the world's finest hour, and all he could think was that he'd give his right arm for a little saliva to make swallowing possible again.

But then this rush, this familiar, all-powerful rush, washing the fear from its origins. And he was standing there alone, oblivious to the world looking in on him by satellite, but still acutely conscious of the importance of the moment. And he was there because it was meant to be. He looked around and all else vanished but this truth. This palpable reality. This tangible high.

"As our honorable representative from Bangladesh so plainly put it," he finally began, "this is indeed a day to be savored and to be grateful for." He smiled as the words began to flow – smiled because it was a great day and because they were finally flowing. "Today marks the day when people of the world officially unite in their efforts to stabilize living conditions on this planet. When people of the world, united as brothers and sisters in the larger scheme of existence – commit themselves to taking the necessary steps to regain control of their precious mother Earth, for the common good of all her children."

He could tell by looking at the expressions that the translations were instantaneous, the current of emotions in synch with his own.

"The French have a saying," he went on. *L'impossible n'est pas français.* Impossible isn't French. Well, it seems to me that today we can conclusively say, humankind is not limited by illusions of the impossible, but is limited only by the scope of its dreams. For today we have seen the realization of a great, impossible dream – the signing of the Constitution that will forever guide the Federation of Earth."

And it wasn't until he had said it, until he had put the period solidly at the end of that long-awaited sentence and basked in it a while, that he allowed himself to wonder if she was there. As the delegation applauded, he scanned the auditorium for her face. No, not her young face, he reminded himself, but the one that had lived and loved and suffered and toiled and rejoiced and earned its creases and wrinkles. But he knew the truth even as he worked on avoiding it.

"I'm sorry, Sir," his secretary had told him contritely, as if sensing his life depended on it. "I can't find Ms. Cagle on the Delegate list... No, Sir, she's not an observer, either. Is there anything else I can – ?" But he'd waved her off like a bothersome fly, instantly reproaching himself for it. What he'd wanted to say was, *Could you just find out if she's still alive?* To which he might have added a *please* or a *thank-you*. But even with the amenities attached, it would have sounded so desperate.

Anyway, he didn't need verification that Katie Cagle was alive. Only six months before, he'd heard she was coming out of retirement to spearhead an educational youth program in Boston. Six months was a long time in the context of potential life changes but, the fact was, he could feel her Earthly presence. Or at least he thought he could. Which got him to thinking about the airline crash two miles from his house one sleepy Sunday afternoon. The day 252 people plunged to their fiery death – he never feeling a twinge. Two hundred and fifty-two people annihilated just two miles from his brain waves and not even a bruise to his psyche. Was it possible that Katie could have left this world and he not felt even the breeze of her passing?

Finishing his speech, he left the podium, reminding himself that everything was possible. The good, the great, and the unspeakable.

He shook a lot of hands that day, more hands in one day than he ever had before, judging by the stiffness of his fingers and the general numbness of his hands. Later that evening, prompted by the loneliness one feels when all emotions have been spent, he downed a club soda at the hotel bar (he'd been clean and sober for years now) and headed for the section of beach reserved for guests – a beach made all the more private by the tight security imposed around its perimeters.

Stepping out onto the beach, RJ couldn't help but note the irony: a world without boundaries – a beach cordoned off. Taking off his shoes, he dug his feet into the sand where they searched in vain for the inner child. The search complete, he walked toward the Mediterranean, stopping to throw off his jacket and unbutton his shirt as his Secret Service agents looked nervously in his direction. Peeling his shirt from his body, he rolled up his pants legs and allowed the waves to play between his toes before slowly making his way into the water, finally plunging in and disappearing beneath the surface.

Barely making a ripple, the waters closed up after him. The air was still, the sea a blue beyond compare.

- 3 -

Katie

HE BURST THROUGH THE WATER like a dolphin on a mission. Young and restlessly alive, he took only a second to gauge his proximity to shore. Swiftly, adeptly, he swam in that direction and, reaching shore, ran for the pile of belongings waiting for him on the sand. Shaking the wet from his long blonde hair, he put on his glasses before taking off his swimming suit. Butt naked now, he threw on his shorts, grabbed his shirt and flip-flops, and ran into his ocean-side apartment through the open patio door.

Things were neat inside, but not excessively so, furniture sparse and early thrift store – a computer, some gadgets, good books, law books, political science, evidence of a working mind. Grabbing a nearby towel, he headed down the hallway and into the bathroom, coming out a second later combing the knots from his hair. His hair tangled too easily, and he told himself he'd probably be better off shaving the whole damn mess, but he wasn't quite ready to part with it. A security thing more than a vanity thing. He needed his hair to stay in touch.

Opening his little black book, he quickly found a number, picked up the phone, and dialed.

She answered almost instantly.

Katie sometimes wondered if the memory of Muriel, her adoptive mother, had anything to do with reality. In conjuring up the image of her face, she was never able to apply anything but a smile to her lips and a twinkle to her eye. Still, Katie's memories were reliable enough and, in the end, she was forced to conclude that her mother was simply one of those rare spirits who came into the world smiling in anticipation of a great and useful life. Even in the weeks before her death, when her suffering was the greatest, Muriel's only thought had been of others. She'd slipped into a semi-coma by the time Katie had come into the room to say goodbye, but had managed somehow to squeeze Katie's fingers as if to tell her in parting not to waste her tears on what was a natural and unavoidable thing.

As a child, Katie had taken Muriel's presence in her life for granted – yet, at another level, had managed to consciously revere her above all others. She was the sunshine of Katie's life, the brightness that lit every room. In later years, Katie would come to appreciate that a beauty as radiant, effervescent, and invincible as her mother's could not be willed or fabricated or embellished, but could only come from the heart, the spirit, and the soul.

Sadly, the memory of Katie's birth mother had quickly faded after the accident, leaving only nuances of a sullen, undemonstrative woman. But, as the image of that mother faded, the picture of her birth father became more distinct. Maternal in ways that her mother wasn't, Katie would always remember the gentleness with which he would wipe her tears, rubbing the moisture into his own cheek as if to soften his skin. Nor could she forget the times he was there to tend to her when she was sick, painting her throat with bitter-tasting medicines, and plying her with mysterious, foul-smelling teas until the beast was either drowned or poisoned, or in some other way obliterated.

With the death of her father, Katie had lost her magic mirror, the one in which she could gaze at herself and know without doubt that she was beautiful. But, on that day, when the door had slammed shut on her young, unsuspecting face, another door had opened and, like an angel from the world beyond, Muriel had walked into her life. And, for this, despite the blow that life had dealt her, she would always be indebted to the hand of fate.

Many years later and, at forty-one, far enough into the heart of life that glasses were becoming something of an imperative, Katie wondered how it came to be that she now sat in this chair, by this window, at this computer, in a place she had once reviled. As a child, she had happily tagged along to her parents' "office", eager to stuff envelopes and win her mother's approval. But, beyond that, the memories of the early days spent in this lonely place were tinged with the darkness of her father's relentless crusade. Who would have guessed that, after Samuel's passing, she herself would put such time and energy into the very Movement that had, in so many ways, stolen her childhood? A Movement that, after Muriel's passing, had meant virtually nothing to her.

The office wasn't much by any standards, though it had markedly softened and mellowed with time. Plants, posters, multi-colored maps of the world, and wildflower bouquets provided enough of a personal touch to give the place a certain charm, and computers, printers and fax machines told of work that went on. *One World* proclaimed one of the larger posters featuring planet Earth, and books crowding the book shelves titillated with subjects ranging from economics to global warming. And in the corner, always in the corner, was the ghost of Samuel, watching her, measuring her progress, or lack thereof, weighing her opinions sharply against his own – while, always at her side, was Muriel, urging her on with the rational arguments and the gentle encouragement that were her trademarks.

The phone rang, interrupting Katie's lapse of focus, and she looked at her co-worker across the room in the hopes that she would pick up the phone. But Luna had her ear phones on, immersed in some secret music, so Katie braced herself and took the call.

"Federation of Earth." She had said the words so many times, they had become a single entity, a piece of rhetoric drowned out by a slurp of coffee and a medley of strokes at the keyboard.

"Hey there! This is RJ Cutter. Who's this?"

"This is Katie," she answered, recognizing the name and groaning internally.

"Katie, hi," he said, oblivious to her darker side. "Just wondering about the Congo. Everything still on?" Done with combing his wet hair, he threw it back onto his shoulders with a sweep of his head – a move he'd perfected over the last few weeks spent on the beach front.

"Everything's still on." Katie motioned to Luna, who took off her earphones to tune in. Cupping her hand over the mouthpiece, Katie whispered, "It's our delegate from sunny California," before going back to RJ to ask, "Is there something I can help you with?" Turning back to Luna, she reiterated. "The kid."

Katie put RJ on speaker phone now and went about her business.

"We're meeting in Barcelona, right?" he continued, aware of having been put on speaker phone and only a little annoyed by it.

"Right," she answered, her eyes squinting at the computer screen. "We'll meet your plane."

"Flight 354, arrives Barcelona at 1:53 p.m."

"It's a full six weeks away. Maybe we should talk closer to departure time."

"Just wanted to make sure you have everything you need from me. You got my registration form, right? Everything filled out okay?"

"Set and ready to go. Assuming you have your passport and visa."

"Right here in front of me."

"You might want to consider taking anti-malarial pills." She was trying to extend herself, to exude a modicum of kindness. She reminded herself that it was the least someone working on behalf of world peace should emote. Still, it wasn't easy putting up with the annoying phone calls, the naiveté, the editorializing, the steady stream of threats. She added with regard to the malaria pills, "You might want to start them early," because she knew it was the right thing to say.

"Mefloquine?" He was right on it. "Just got my prescription filled. So what are your thoughts about getting vaccinated against yellow fever? I'm not keeping you, am I?"

"I'll probably pass on it." *Naive, but not uninformed*, she told herself.

"I know it's not a must, but I think I'll get one myself. You never can be too sure, right? Think I'll get a dose of immune globin Hepatitis A vaccine while I'm at it. I kind of cling to my well-being – know what I mean?"

Not uninformed, but increasingly annoying.

RJ waited for Katie to speak and, when she chose to continue typing instead, he filled the void.

"Okay then."

"Talk to you soon." She took him off of speaker, glad to be rid of him. Turning to Luna now, she said, "He drives me nuts."

"He's eager," Luna countered. "Eager is good, remember? Besides, he's our one and only official American delegate. You ought to be down on your knees worshiping him."

But Katie wasn't about to get down on her knees and worship anyone, much the less some young and hopelessly naive believer from Southern California. Let Luna worship him – she who was capable of worshiping anything that remotely smacked of humanity. Let the Earth muffin wearing the bangles and bracelets and the soulful expression in her big brown eyes be the first to put her arm around him and welcome him to the fold.

Katie stared at the screen saver on her computer, now flashing, *Federation by the Year 2015,* and wondered how many more times they'd have to revise that figure. She looked for her glasses, finally finding them around her neck, put them on, then took them off again to rub away the headache starting behind her eyes.

Getting right to the heart of the headache, Luna offered, "I thought you were going to get rid of that thing."

Katie looked down at the wedding band she'd never been able to part with. "Can't get it off," she replied.

"Soap and water. Worked for me."

After a moment, Katie said, as if it were relevant, "Last night, I dreamed there were two moons in the sky."

And just when Luna was about to attempt a little unsolicited dream analysis, into the room walked James

Norwalk. A thickset man in his late seventies, he was looking a little green around the gills. "I think I'm going to head home," he said, creasing the edge of a notebook between his fingers.

"Not feeling well?" Katie asked, seeing the answer in the hue of his skin.

"You'll let me know if there's anything important."

"Of course." Despite the natural concern she felt for the man's health, Katie always felt more comfortable when he wasn't around and found it easy to encourage him to take his leave. He was getting too old for all of this anyway.

An old cohort of Katie's father's, Norwalk had long been the financial force behind the Movement, content in his later years to play golf with his peers, tend to his Japanese garden, and be kept abreast of activities on a quarterly basis. After Samuel's death, he had reluctantly taken the helm – never mind that the captain's hat was a size too big for his head. At least he was there in the flesh, giving the appearance of stability and forward momentum. And, thanks in large part to Katie who had, by default, also taken her place in the new regime, the office would remain largely functional.

Norwalk lingered an awkward moment for no better reason than that he was by nature a lingerer, when the phone finally broke the silence. Norwalk took the opportunity to make his exit, while Katie, on her end, made no move to answer the phone.

"I kind of doubt that it's the kid again," Luna said after a couple of rings. "He usually gives it at least twenty-four hours."

"I'm sure you're right," Katie agreed, not without a hint of sarcasm. "Probably just another fanatic."

Katie's demons were a mystery to Luna, and she'd given up long ago on figuring out what possessed her to be both driven to do the world a service, and so apathetic to the process. But it was good enough that she was a kind and essentially sweet-spirited friend, and Luna would gladly leave it at that. So, instead of belaboring the point, she quickly changed gears and dove into her purse on a quest to subsidize her habit.

"Don't even ask," Katie pre-empted.

Luna slapped the radio in a futile attempt to get it to come on. "Get the motherload," she said, handing Katie a ten-dollar bill.

Katie got on her bike and waved at the neighbor she knew wouldn't wave back. He was a harmless sort, just didn't like his boat rocked, which meant he'd rather they took their enterprise elsewhere. To Jupiter, for instance. Didn't like her bike either. It was an eyesore.

She passed the mailman who waved back as if he had no choice in the matter. But Katie was used to that, and she took off down the street, if not a song in her heart, at least the promise of a couple of burritos reminding her why life was worth living. Pedaling up the hill was a chore, but the blood pumped to her brain gave her needed clarity. Turning her head toward the azure of the sky, now melting into the gray-green of the mountains, she reminded herself that she lived in paradise.

It had been the right decision, that decision she'd made so long ago – to move back to Colorado to stay. She'd made the decision after Samuel's passing, though not in his honor. As impassioned as Samuel had been for the cause of world government, he'd never been its most convincing proponent – though what he lacked in charm and charisma, he certainly made up for in drive and determination. But it was hard for anyone, much the less for Katie, to find inspiration from a man whose obsessive desire to mold the world into a peaceful and well-oiled machine was driven by intellectual obsession, and not by a burning love for humankind.

What had Muriel ever seen in Samuel beyond the mutual dream? Katie asked herself the question as she pedaled her bicycle, listening to the familiar rattle of the chain under her feet – the rattle that, oddly enough, always gave her an agreeable sense of security. The sound of gears in motion, of life that goes on. Fortified by this feeling, and by the sun on her shoulders, she let herself be transported to the day when Muriel died.

For Katie, painfully vulnerable in the way that only youth can be, that particular spring would be a bitter one. Even so, no one was more astounded than Samuel when Muriel's cancer was proclaimed, no one more devastated when she passed away. She had been for so many years his rock, his inspiration, his salvation. She had also been his nemesis and, in that place of torment where his devils dwelled, she continued to dwarf him, to outshine him, and to exceed him. Always ahead of him in the race, she had even beat him into the next world.

Devastated by the loss of her strongest supporter, Katie waited in vain for the comfort and assurance that a father's arms might bring. She waited, finally realizing that expectation brought with it more pain than did certitude. Armed with that awareness, she put a stop to the waiting.

As time passed, an embittered Samuel began to call upon her to fill in at the office after school. Stuff envelopes and order office supplies, make coffee and water the plants, dust the pictures, stack the magazines, and, above all, reinforce his flagging ego. Katie obeyed her father's orders reluctantly. In time, she performed by rote, without meaning, but also without rancor. She understood that her father's ambitions were commendable. After all, they had been her mother's ambitions too. Still, she questioned Samuel's motives, questioning at the same time whether motives were of any importance in the scheme of things.

There were brief moments when Samuel seemed to be reaching out to her, to show evidence of a budding fatherly pride. But, if the feeling was genuine, its existence was short-lived, displaced by the blossoming of Katie's own persona. In the end, it was Katie herself who would come between her and the father she would never fully fathom. And, to the degree that Katie began to trust herself, Samuel began to distrust his daughter. So began a cold and despotic behavior pattern from which he would never deviate.

It had been hard to gauge at first, this evolution into darkness. Mystified as she was by his ways, Katie had always managed to accept and endure his aloofness, telling herself that genius had its imperfections. This was, in fact, the approach that others in the Movement took to cushion themselves against the assault of Samuel's increasingly unpredictable personality. Katie often toyed with thoughts of running away, convinced that, in mourning her absence, he would come to his senses and fill her world with the tenderness for which she desperately longed. But, fully aware that she was all he really had, she couldn't bring herself to leave him – not in spirit, not completely. Not until the day he finally crossed the line.

She'd been sitting at the kitchen table, staring at the rain slapping against the window, oblivious to the dinner that the cook had put in front of her.

In France, where Katie would spend the greater part of her adolescence, the rain was a constant companion, lamenting alongside her as only a friend could do. France had been Muriel's idea, the move executed at the nadir of Samuel's popularity in the eyes of the U.S. government. Distance would be good for Samuel, Muriel had argued, and Katie would have a chance to get back in touch with her roots and refresh her waning French. The idea had been a sound one, and they had kept a home there, along with their States-side residence, even after Muriel's death.

Katie had been mesmerized by the rain, enraptured by the intensity and magnitude of the downpour. Then, the maid had left, the rain had abated, and Katie had finally been forced to consider the plate in front of her, noting with dismay the Brussels sprouts nestled against the single slice of poached salmon.

At fourteen, Katie fully understood that others less fortunate than herself often went hungry in this world. But she had trouble understanding the connection between forcing a hated food into an unwilling stomach, and feeding the hungry miles from her dinner table. And so, with the maid out of the room, she had quickly dumped the hated green monsters into the garbage can, burying them as deeply as she could. Then she had sat back down and prodded at the salmon and watched the rain weave its way down the window pane.

When Samuel entered the room a few moments later, she felt her stomach tighten, then relax as he took a seat across from her and began to eat his own meal.

"It's really pouring," she managed, longing, for reasons she couldn't fathom, to throw her arms around his neck.

She was willing him to smile, willing it with all her youthful energy, but also knowing that smiles and Samuel were of late mutually exclusive, to the degree that when his lips did manage to form the shape in question, the benefactor was usually somewhat repulsed or mystified by it, as if the smile had been unwittingly plastered under the wrong nose. But on this occasion, there was no smile, forced or otherwise, his pitiless eyes slowly turning to the vacancy on her plate, his face void of any discernible expression.

After a long silence, gnawing silence, Samuel said simply, "I see you ate your Brussels sprouts."

She could only hope that the smile on her face would not betray her growing inner terror.

"You did eat them, didn't you?" he persisted in a tone that bordered oddly on forbearance.

"What do you mean? I told you. I did."

He paused, then asked flatly, "Where are they?"

Looking for a quick defense, Katie answered, "Where would they be ten minutes after you've swallowed them?"

"Be truthful, do you hear me?" he shouted. "The truth, do you understand?"

But the only truth Katie was in touch with was her right to protect herself, and she defended that truth now with all the courage her young spirit could muster. "I'm not lying!" she shouted. "Why don't you ever believe me?"

This seemed to quiet him at first, and Katie noted for future reference that shouting seemed to have a placating effect on him. He resumed his eating, slowly at first, then at a more normal pace, at which point Katie's stomach finally began to settle. Again, she searched for a way into benign conversation, but was quickly thwarted when, as if struck by sudden inspiration, Samuel put down his fork, got up from the table, and took a stand by the garbage can.

Katie waited. *I know where you hid the body*, she could hear him thinking.

"You didn't throw them in the garbage, did you?" he taunted her.

"No, Daddy. Really. I swear. I didn't." Katie noted with detached interest that she had called him *Daddy* and not *Samuel*, as she usually did, and she found it oddly interesting that *Daddy* was apparently reserved, not for moments of filial affection, but for moments that gave rise to contrition and desperation.

But, before she could add tears to her plea of innocence, or change her plea to guilty and beg for mercy, Samuel had grabbed the garbage can and, in one fluid motion, dumped the contents all over the kitchen floor. Katie watched as milk cartons fell onto the tile, belching and dribbling their soured remnants, and egg shells and coffee grounds converged with crumpled newspapers like paint splattered on an unsuspecting canvas. And she noted with that odd sense of disconnection that always seemed to overtake her in times of crisis, that there was a single yellow crayon that rolled across the room and came to rest at her feet. A single yellow crayon that seemed to say, *Don't worry, Katie. Life isn't as bad as it seems. Just color it yellow. You'll see.* And, of course, she noted, as did Samuel, those perfectly-shaped miniature cabbages that lay unscathed at the heart of the exotic pile of rubbish. Those formidable, indomitable Brussels sprouts.

Strictly opposed to physical violence, Samuel betrayed the anger that boiled at the depths of his being only through the telling trembling of his hands. After a moment of this, he turned and left the room, left the mess on the floor, left her sitting there as if she inherently belonged among the coffee grounds and the egg shells and the soured milk.

It was a long time before Katie got up from the table, feeling little emotion beyond a growing emptiness. Picking the crayon off the floor, she studied it, wondering how it had ever found its way into the garbage, as she was well beyond the crayon years. She imagined the crayon's journey, from factory line to this very moment, its noble mission finally complete. For the first time that day, a smile crossed Katie's lips, and she decided that yellow would, from now on, be her favorite color, Brussels sprouts her most hated vegetable, and lying her least favorite refuge. But, in that moment, she knew she had won, for she realized that, for all his harshness and aloofness, there was nothing Samuel could do to bring greater harm to her soul than had already been inflicted upon it on that day.

But that was many years ago, and now Samuel was gone, and she was in the here and now and off her bike at Jake's Burritos. Two burritos, one without cilantro, the other with double the sour cream. Luna liked to live dangerously.

Thinking back on the experience, which Katie would do at regular intervals throughout her life, she wasn't able to fully pinpoint what was going through her head when it happened. Maybe she was thinking about Muriel, about how much she missed the sound of her laughter. Or of Luna, of how uncommon it was to have found a friend so wise and true. But there was always the possibility that she was thinking about her overdue car payment, or why Mark had left her for another woman, or whether it even mattered to her. She did remember, however, what went through her mind when she heard the explosion. Her bicycle had lurched forward, the handlebars shaking in unison with her brain, and then she had thought to herself, *Damn.*

Just that. *Damn.*

Which included the range of emotions that one felt when one believed the bomb had finally been dropped on the world.

When one believed the beginning of the end was finally here, and humankind had finally lost its collective sanity. When nuclear holocaust was finally upon the planet. The very thing she had – on behalf of humanity but, more accurately, on behalf of the ghosts that still haunted her – worked so diligently to prevent.

She stopped her bike – or did it come to a stop as it hit the curb? – and she let herself drop to the sidewalk – or was she catapulted there? Unaware of the three-inch gash above her knee, she heard the sirens and saw the smoke and realized it wasn't a nuclear explosion at all.

And then she saw that the smoke was coming from her building.

She managed to walk her bike the rest of the way, staring all the while at the gaping hole that had been blown into the side of the building where the office was located. A fire, apparently contained to that one side, still burned at the heart of an eerie quiet, over which the sounds of public radio could be heard. Katie looked and listened, her ears and eyes doing their best to take in the overall picture.

A rebel ultimatum gave Zairian leader, Mobutu Sese Seko, until Sunday to resign, the radio announcer reported, *a demand Mobutu summarily rejected. The military governor of Kinshasa, General Amela Lokima, described the capital as being in chaos and implored its five million residents to be calm. An atmosphere of panic reigns among Kinshasa's men and women, Lokima said in a television address. The most fantastic rumors, according to which the city of Kinshasa would soon fall to the rebellion, are gaining ground..."*

All of that was well and horrible, but what about her friend? And just as she was thinking that perhaps her legs would take her where she needed to go, the police car pulled up, followed by the fire truck and ambulance. And anyway,

she knew it was too late. The radio was working, and Luna
was dead.

4

Sagan

THAT SAME DAY
TOPEKA, KANSAS

JACQUES LEGRAND SAGAN, known to his friends as Sagan (rhymes with pagan, he liked to say), opened the front door of what he commonly referred to as his humble hacienda, as if to greet his own beloved mother. Handsome in a broken-nosed sort of way, he was a virile-looking teddy bear with intelligent eyes that did their best to conceal an inherent vulnerability. He wore his well-established middle-age with a certain panache, the grin on his face the product of an irrepressible exuberance for life, amplified by a little too much vino, a glass of which he currently held in his hand.

It never mattered too much to him who rang the doorbell. Whether it was the mailman or the paper boy, he was willing to make conversation. Boredom could do that to you – make you see the lure of friendship in even the coldest eye. Today his visitors happened to be a couple of women – door-to-door evangelists, as evidenced by the Bible clutched protectively to the breast of the shorter one.

"Ladies! How are you?" Sagan greeted them, sloshing a little wine at their feet for emphasis.

There was a moment of reckoning on the part of both women, a brief hesitation. But then Sagan's smile bore fruit, and the taller one pulled a folded sheet of paper from her carry-all bag. She managed to unfold it without tearing it – not an easy trick, given its paper-thin status, and started to hold the picture up for viewing. But just then the run-down bicycle perched precariously by the side of the front door came crashing down between her and the doorway. She extricated her foot from its spokes and looked up at Sagan with some frustration.

Noblesse oblige, Sagan came through to avenge her, kicking the bicycle aside, then topping off the gesture with a generous smile and yet another kick that sent the bicycle sliding across the porch.

A little uncertainly, the woman held up the picture, and Sagan took stock of it – a WASP-ish-looking family, seated on a bench amid a host of heavenly creatures in what must have been someone's rendition of the great hereafter.

"Wouldn't you like to know that a place like this is waiting for you after you die?" asked the shorter one.

Not one to take a serious question lightly, Sagan gave the issue some reflection, taking another sip of wine in the process, letting it glide around inside his mouth and under his tongue, savoring every molecule, the better to contemplate heaven by.

"You do speak English, don't you?" the taller evangelist finally asked, prompted by his long silence.

"May I?" Sagan took the picture from the woman's hands for better viewing, sipping his wine and studying the picture with apparent intensity.

"Because you have a slight accent," the woman added.

"Ah!" Carefully, Sagan handed the picture back to her. "Well, I suppose I do have a little Chateau Lafitte in my ancestral gene pool. Ergo, I like to consider myself a citizen of the world." In fact, Sagan's father was French, his mother American, and he had always felt as torn between two worlds as a person of divided allegiances possibly could. But he had given up the tug of war a long time ago, figuring he was – mongrel heritage notwithstanding – nothing more or less than human. "How about you ladies?" he asked.

When neither of them responded, Sagan remembered that, in fact, it was still his turn. "The picture! Yes. Well. They look..." But, though Sagan preferred honesty to pretense, he also preferred to blend tactfulness with directness whenever possible, especially where women were concerned. Therefore, he would have to weigh his answer carefully.

The shorter one filled in before his answer hit the scales. "...happy?"

"...lobotomized," he countered without thinking. There. Now he'd done it. Not at all what he had intended to say. "But, of course, I'm sure I'd be missing the whole point. It's just that there's this lifeless expression on the woman's face ... is that an oxymoron – *lifeless expression*?"

Then, as if struck by a sudden inspiration, Sagan held up a rigid index finger, indicating that no one should move a muscle, and headed down the hallway toward the kitchen.

Sagan had always been both a man's man and a ladies' man and yet, in the end, belonged to no one but himself. He had this uncanny sense of timing – being a journalist, it helped. It also helped when you were just trying to make it through life unscathed. He always seemed to know when to joke, when to be serious, when to put his fist down, when to put a friendly hand on your shoulder, and when to run a fingertip across your cheek. Recently, though, he'd had this feeling he was losing his touch, wondering in darker moments if he were seeing the beginnings of a steady downward spiral. The problem with middle age, he concluded, was not middle age itself, but the fact that it foreshadowed old age, decline, and… god-forbid, senility. But he wiped the thought from his brain, reminding himself that with his swashbuckling face and smile that could still knock the pants right off of you, he had no trouble finding women. That had to be the measure of something, though he wasn't quite sure of what. In fact, women had always flocked to him. And he, in turn, had loved every single one of them with an urgent passion, though seldom passionately enough to remember their faces the next day, much the less invite them to stay for breakfast.

Somewhere in all of that senselessness, he met Katie. And finally he had a point of reference – a yardstick by which to measure the woman of his own heretofore-indefinable dreams. Still, in truth, it had nothing to do with measure or degree, more to do with that elusive, unexplainable connection which two people occasionally share, and which seems to be predicated on some mystic quality more profound than the mere physical or mental attributes of either party.

He thought of her as he made his way into the kitchen – thought of her as she was then, thought of her as she was now. He was older than she, ten years or so, not enough to make a federal case of. He'd met her when she was barely seventeen, and had fallen instantly, reverently, in love with her. How sweet she had looked in that loose-fitting red sweater and lopsided grin and that crazy-curly black hair. How utterly unlike anyone he'd ever known. Dark-skinned, quasi-beautiful, and oddly inviting in her own unwelcoming way, the boundaries of her heart so clearly defined – a brave crusader, shooting arrows at his soul when he ventured in too close to her guarded territory. Interestingly enough, unlike the other women toward whom he seemed to gravitate, he wasn't physically possessed by her, not immediately, anyway. She was never to him what the others were – adversaries in the war of love, wielding their own special brand of erogenous weaponry. No, Katie was a face, a heart, a soul – a soul that would eventually, and after much effort on his part, warm to him and grow to trust him, though not to return the depth of his love. And as for her body... well, suffice it to say, that particular territory had never been explored.

Sagan was not the marrying kind which, in view of his romantic predicament, was just as well. In a way, it was comfortable, this arrangement he had with Katie. This unlikely friendship, as she called it. A letter here and there. A kiss on the cheek when they saw each other. An occasional crossing of work paths, and a slight overlap of conscience. For, strip away the bon vivant, the womanizer – even the consummate journalist and skilled photographer – and at the heart of it was Sagan the mere human being, the man whose wine-sodden, life-weary façade betrayed a wine-sodden, life-weary interior. Not that he didn't cherish a profound wish for peace, or more specifically, an end to violence and suffering. And not that he had any inherent objection to the idea of world government. No, in fact, he wished the world harmony in whatever way the world could find harmony for itself, much in the same breath that he wished himself a good night's sleep, food on the table, and ample wine in the cellar. It's just that he was less political than he was socially analytical, and less of an activist than an after-dinner philosopher. In short, he was content to let others do the caring, at least out there on the global stage. And anyway, he couldn't help but wonder about people who worked too hard to lift the suffering masses – wondered just why they were so eager to drain their own energies to achieve the impossible, suspecting it had less to do with benevolence than with simple co-dependency.

Putting Katie out of his mind, Sagan headed down the hallway, past rows of framed black and white photographs that in some fashion or another depicted the plight and pathos of humanity and which were, in fact, the record of Sagan's life as a freelance journalist – as one critic put it, *a vivid and haunting testament to his patient and perceptive eye.*

Sagan grabbed a postcard from its magnetized place on the refrigerator door and hurried out of the room with it, making short headway before turning back on his heels to get a refill of the wine sitting on the kitchen counter. Making his way back to the ladies in waiting, he began to whistle. "Why do you whistle?" his mother used to tease him. "Is it because you're such a happy child?" But, both then and now, it had little to do with happiness and more to do with tension – something about the teapot coming to a boil and the steam needing to be released.

"I'm back," he announced, as if there were a need to. He noted that he was out of breath and told himself again he'd better get on that diet he'd been talking about for the last two months – the meat and potatoes one that claimed to hold its own against the others.

Sagan held the postcard up for the women to see – a photograph of a cloudless sky overlooking snow-capped mountains encircling a profusion of wildflowers. The relevance wasn't immediately clear to the women, and they stared, first at the postcard, then, alternately, at Sagan.

"Now, this –" Sagan explained, smacking the postcard for emphasis and once again spilling his wine onto their shoes, "– this is my idea of heaven. Sunshine. Mountains. A swim in the lake with not so much as your favorite shoes on. A ripe and lovely woman by your side – no shoes for her either. A glass of

Bordeaux ...” But there was still confusion written on their faces, and Sagan backpedaled to clarify. “The San Juan Mountains, Colorado. Much prettier than Topeka, don’t you think? You wouldn’t have any pictures of hell in your handbag, would you? Because I’m seriously starting to wonder if Topeka is it.” The bait had been floundering around the lake bottom for too long now, and Sagan decided to reel it in. “Would you care to come in for a cup of tea? We could look for common ground. Discuss our minor philosophical differences...”

But God and the nuances of heaven were not up for discussion. The women weren’t hooked. If they’d taken the bait, they’d neatly eaten it and deftly left the hook behind. They didn’t come in. Sagan was disappointed, but not fatally so. He shut the door behind them and took a moment to lean against the doorway. As if in afterthought, he looked at the postcard again, then turned it over to read the other side. His disappointment yielded to a smile, then to sweet melancholy, as he contemplated the words that were written there. Slowly, he finished his wine.

5

Great Hope

(THE SAN JUAN MOUNTAINS)
ONE MONTH LATER
MAY 16, 1997

 *THE SAN JUAN MOUNTAINS* are the youngest and most rugged mountains in the Rocky Mountain range. Once the sacred hunting grounds of the Ute Indians, this awe-inspiring stretch of craggy rocks and resplendent greenery that boasts snow-capped peaks in the middle of summer, has often been compared to the Swiss Alps.

Nestled somewhere in the heartland of this pristine paradise is Great Hope, a small town named by its founder for the belief he held that the town would be a seat of commerce and culture for a new and expanding territory. Unfortunately, it missed the mark, as did the railroad that bypassed it. Gone are the brothels but, apart from that perceived improvement, most of the original buildings are still standing, many of them artfully and painstakingly renovated. The citizens of Great Hope covet their roots so intensely that the entire town is listed on the National Register of Historic Districts. To walk its streets is to take a step back in time. To gaze at the scenery that surrounds it is to merge with eternity.

Wouldn't you like to know that a place like this is waiting for you after you die? The question came back to him as he rolled into the purple-green heart of the San Juan Mountains. To Sagan, there was no finer spot on Earth, no sweeter place in heaven. Sure, part of it was because she lived there, but where that fact ended and the landscape began, he couldn't say. Were it not for the fact that he wouldn't have a reason to come visit, he would have moved there himself. But, in some strange way, the meetings and the partings were what made it special. Besides, he was kind of invested in Topeka.

His car – a beater that refused to do more than 10 miles an hour on the incline – was grunting and groaning as Sagan urged it onward, and Sagan began to whistle as if to distance himself from the urgency of making it up the mountain. He tuned the radio to international news, also a nervous habit, managing to successfully ignore the 4-wheel drives, trucks, RVs, and bicyclists now passing him with abandon.

The question on his mind was this: *What's new in the Congo?* Determined to find out, he worked the defective radio with the finesse of a safe-cracker, finally landing on the station that would tell him.

..Rebel troops are advancing toward Kinshasa, the radio announcer informed him, and Sagan stopped whistling to listen in. *Zairian President, Mobutu Sese Seko, relinquished his power on Friday, and headed into exile ... But with Mobutu fleeing the country, no one knows who his immediate successor will be. Laurent Kabila and his rebels have captured most of the country since October. Sources say the United States has offered Kabila a full $10 million in assistance to hold elections after his expected takeover of Zaire ... The United States' position is clear, said President Clinton. We want to see a transition to a genuine democracy.*

Sagan rounded the top of the mountain, put the car in neutral, and coasted the rest of the way, building up enough speed to pass the same 4-wheel drives, trucks, RVs, and bicyclists that had passed him so effortlessly on the way up.

Ahead of the pack now, he blazed a trail of exhaust fumes into the outskirts of Great Hope.

Katie rode her bicycle into the parking lot and hopped off. Resting her bicycle against the side of the building, she took a bag of apples out of the bicycle basket, simultaneously noting how well the bike fit in with the partially blown-out wall. Repairs had been done to both, but neither seemed improved by the effort. Still they functioned, they served a purpose. They survived.

Going into the building, Katie cast a puzzled backward glance at the car parked in the street out front. Although she wasn't entirely sure about it, the parallel parking job gave rise to a growing suspicion. But she quickly put this out of her mind, certain that he – Sagan, if her hunch was correct – would have called first. Or would have somehow assured himself that she was going to be around. There were no romantic ties between them; still, their friendship demanded it.

At her desk now, Katie turned up the music on the radio, then opened the bag of apples and took one out. Her hands were shaking slightly, to which she paid little attention. It happened once in a while, this nervous ripple, an after-effect of the bombing (according to her psychologist), nothing to be overly concerned about. Time would take care of it. That and a prescription for a mild but slightly-addictive sedative, which Katie did her best not to abuse. Polishing the apple on her shirt sleeve, she was about to put it in her mouth in a hunger only remotely related to appetite, when she heard muted conversation from the next room.

She turned down the radio, and heard Norwalk say, "Sam trusted you." Taking her apple and her curiosity with her, she went to listen by the open door and smiled at the sound of Sagan's voice. How long had it been since she'd heard that deep, guttural voice – that friendly growl? A year, she figured, maybe even a year and a half, and the sound of it filled her with the closest thing to joy that she'd felt in a long time. She'd come to count on him, she realized, to look forward to his short-lived but impassioned visits, revitalized and refreshed by them, the way one felt at the onslaught and passing of a storm long overdue.

"But why the Congo?" Sagan was saying. "Why not Nepal? Bangladesh? I could name you ten countries off the top of my head that would make more sense right now than the Congo."

"Maybe..." Norwalk came back so slowly that Sagan was tempted to fill in for him. "But," Norwalk finally continued, "they're all too.. ." He searched for the word, coming up with it only after some fruitless gesticulating. "...*beholding* to the United States. Visas would be denied across the board, just the way they were the last time we tried to plan a bona fide constitutional convention."

The last two times, Katie mentally corrected, taking another bite of her apple, the juice squirting liberally over her fingers and dribbling its way down the sleeves of her shirt. Disasters, both of them, in terms of morale, and in terms of monies lost by third-world delegates. A total of nearly 1,500 delegates turned away at the last possible moment. The conferences foiled, the Movement itself temporarily disabled.

"The government of the Congo is behind our Movement," Norwalk went on in that steady, unnervingly deliberate manner of his, "regardless of U.S. sentiment. I told you, didn't

I? They're providing the Parliamentary Palace for our use. Room for at least a thousand delegates. It's all set." And then he added as if, in the end, it were the only thing that really mattered, "Anyway, it's too late to call it off now."

Sagan recoiled. "I don't see how you can talk about anything being all set. The country's in chaos, for God's sake. Have you even listened to the news in the last few days? As we sit here debating the issue, Laurent Kabila and his rebels have taken Kinshasa!"

"We're not talking about Zaire, Sagan, we're talking about the Republic of the Congo."

"Come on, James. You know as well as I do that Brazzaville sits right across the river. Overwhelmed with Zairian refugees, at the very least."

"Most of whom will be going home as soon as order is restored in Zaire. And besides, I know Kabila personally. He's a supporter. We have nothing to fear."

"We have nothing to fear? Are you crazy as well as totally fucking nuts?"

Katie smiled as Sagan slipped at the edge of his composure.

"How can you say that?" Sagan continued. "As if you aren't perfectly goddamn aware the situation is...," and then he stopped to collect himself, breathing and clearing his throat, and trying to come at it from a different angle.

Norwalk took the opportunity to fill the gap. "A little uncertain? What would you have us do? Cower at every threat of conflict?"

"I wasn't going to say a little uncertain," Sagan said, throwing tact and composure to the wind. "I was going to say, a little fucking volatile."

"The fact is, we'll be far better off with Laurent Kabila across the border than with Mobutu still in power. The man was a cancer on the face of the African continent."

Katie finished the apple, core, seeds, and all, Samuel's waste-not-want-not mentality taking a sudden front seat in her mind.

"Make that the face of humanity and I'm with you all the way," she heard Sagan rebut. "But that's not the point. Okay. Let me put it as bluntly as possible. There's no fucking way I can support this thing. No fucking way."

"You can't?"

"I can't."

"You mean you won't."

"I mean I won't."

Taking stock of the fact that his own argument had failed and opting now for histrionics, Norwalk did his best to shout, "This is revolution, Sagan! Revolution!" But instead of intimidating or inspiring Sagan with his artificially impassioned rhetoric, Norwalk managed only to give rise to concerns for his own health. Sagan took in the shouting, visions of Norwalk having a heart attack playing in his head.

"Calm down, James," Sagan said, putting a hand on his shoulder to settle him.

Norwalk calmed down almost on command, reflecting a moment before adding, "A bloodless revolution. But you know that."

"I do, James. I do."

"Luna's death was a terrible tragedy, Sagan. We were all devastated by it. But the risk has always been there, and there isn't much we can do now but move forward. It's what Sam would have wanted."

In the eerie silence that always followed any reference to Luna's death, Katie found the opportune moment to enter the room. But Sagan and Norwalk were so engrossed in each other's eyes now, so absorbed in weighing the depth of each other's commitment to either side of the argument, that neither of them noticed her. Normally, she wouldn't have minded, but right now the oversight was nipping pointedly at her self-esteem. For reasons she wasn't quite in touch with, she felt minimized.

"I understand what you're saying," Sagan finally said, unmoved by the mention of Samuel's name, but willing to go back to square one to make his point if he had to. "But I want to reiterate, just for the record –"

But he faltered at the feel of something in the air, some vaguely perceptible change, some warmly familiar wave of energy, a fragrance perhaps, and soon his eye had caught sight of her. He stood to greet her, his mood instantly lifted. "Katie!" he exclaimed, immediately drawn to her side. "Salut!" He kissed her once on each cheek and, exercising the French he seldom got to use except in conversations with himself, asked, "Ça va?"

But Katie ignored the French. Going for the meat of it, she said, "Did you get a new car?"

She had always had her eye on the little house in the aspen grove and, after the divorce, she had liquidated her savings and made the down payment. It was a dream come true, coming, ironically, on the tail of the hideous nightmare of divorce. A dream come true without the benefit of jubilation. And it wasn't until long afterward, when she felt again the fragile stirrings of contentment, that she realized she had spent the last two years in a cocoon, deeply and desperately depressed.

Sagan ran his hand across the front door, deep red like the rest of the house and, like the rest of the house, needing a little touch-up.

"Do you still have some of that paint in the garage?" he asked her as she slipped her key in the door.

"I think so."

She entered the house and Sagan followed. He loved this first moment, the moment of entering. Of taking in all the pieces of her life, strewn about the counter tops, posted on the bulletin board, haphazardly stuck in a vase, left to idle on the floor, thrown irreverently in a waste basket. All that was Katie was in this house. And he absorbed it, his affection fueled by it, his longing renewed by it.

She led him to the kitchen, where she kicked off her shoes and quickly put a kettle of water on to boil. Then she opened the refrigerator, standing in front of it as if to decide their mutual fate. "I've got some fresh pickles," she said.

He nodded approvingly.

"You want a sandwich?" she asked.

"With a pickle," he answered.

She's amazing, he told himself as she set about making the sandwich. *The way she works that knife; the way she manages to get that pickle out of the jar without disturbing the others; the way she stands, her feet barely touching the linoleum.* But then he reminded himself that he was raving, that her aura had colored his own, that it was so bright that he was blinded by the light, unable to see a goddamn thing. And that, in fact, Katie, above all others, was only human. Sometimes pretty desperately so. Moreover, it wasn't her perfection, but her very human-ness, that so attracted him to her.

He was back to Earth with both feet when he took the sandwich from her hand. She was a friend. Nothing more. *It is written*, he told himself for the hundredth time. He looked out the picture window for signs of life outside of Katie's kitchen, and found it in the springtime splendor of the mountains.

"I'm sure the FBI is working on it," he said, going back to an earlier conversation.

"Like the FBI really cares what happens to any of us," Katie said, falling into a chair and curling her legs up under her. "The thing that makes it so hard to live with is that it might have been anyone – one of Samuel's old enemies – he had plenty of them, you know – or a die-hard nationalist, or a right-wing extremist, maybe." She looked into Sagan's eyes, that profound in-your-face stare that always stirred his soul and got him wondering if she was starting to care for him. But he knew she wasn't. She was simply gauging her audience, wiggling her finger in the water before she jumped on in. "I'm scared," she said, knowing he was waiting for her to spit it all out. "Sometimes I –"

"Sometimes you what? Tell me, Katie."

Katie took a bite of sandwich, fighting the tears of fear and anger that burned in her eyes.

"You have a right to be frightened, you know. As a matter of fact, you have an obligation to be frightened."

Fear an obligation? Happiness or financial security or emotional fulfillment – those she could understand being obligated to, or striving for, at the least. But fear? But she was way off track. Staring into his eyes, she forced her mind back into his playing field. It was then that she confessed, "It doesn't make me happy to discover that I'm a coward."

"Oh, Katie, please. You're hardly a coward."

Katie shrugged him off, his encouragement and good cheer not hitting the mark. The kettle whistled and, glad for the distraction, Katie said, "You want some tea?"

Sagan nodded. He hated tea, but liked to watch her pour it.

Katie turned off the fire under the kettle and poured two steaming cups. "Peppermint okay?"

"Sure," he said. He hated peppermint, but would drink the poison willingly.

She doesn't want to be comforted, Sagan realized as he absent-mindedly turned to sifting through the junk mail at the center of the kitchen table – *mostly requests for donations*, he noted. And in the midst of it all, one of his own letters to Katie – bulky, crumpled, maybe even well read.

By the time Katie came back to the table, his mind had drifted back to the Congo, and he was working on the case he'd been building for the last two weeks. "You're not planning on going to the Congo, are you?" he asked, not particularly pleased with his opening statement.

When Katie failed to answer, Sagan found himself adding, "Because if you are, I have to tell you – I won't be there to protect you."

"No one's asking you to be. Anyway, I can't exactly miss out on this thing. Not after –" she stopped mid-sentence and started again. "How could I possibly stay behind?"

"Just do like me. Don't get on the plane. Anyway, what makes you think this convention's going to get any further than the last couple attempts? Don't you even give a damn what happens to you anymore? You're crazy, you know." He hadn't intended for it to come out that way, but there it was. "Why don't you do something else for a living?" he went on, because now he was on a roll and, as such, quite unstoppable. "Something less hazardous to your health? Do you want to end up like Luna? Is that it?"

She was shooting daggers at him now, but there were signs of uncertainty behind the anger, and he knew it, and it inspired him to go on.

"Because Muriel lives on in your soul, is that it? Because you feel responsible for her dream? I think even Muriel would have said enough is enough."

"No, she wouldn't have."

This was followed by a long, tea-drinking interlude, neither of them prepared to utter words that might lead to further confrontation. Finally, Katie decided to pour more boiling water into her cup and then, failing to ask, into his.

Sagan put his hand over his cup to indicate that he'd had enough, withdrawing it in a flash when Katie poured the water anyway. Her hands were unsteady and the stream hit the side of the cup, splashing onto the tablecloth.

"You're shaking," he said. No detective work there.

"It's new."

"Ah! Well, we'll have to watch it then, won't we?"

Katie took a sip of her tea, steadying the cup with both hands.

"I got your postcard," he said, changing the subject, his eyes still on her shaking hands.

"A useful tool when you have nothing to say."

"When you have nothing to say, you say nothing in as many words as possible. It's the code I live by."

"Don't be modest, Sagan. It doesn't become you. You're talented and you know it. Luna always thought of you as some sort of Ernest Hemingway."

"You shared my letters with Luna?" It was a reproach.

"Your stories. Your articles. Anyway, why shouldn't I have shared them with her? It's not like they were love letters." Her defensiveness was showing and she knew it. But the battle was ceremonial – a ritualistic, platonic courtship that had to be played out in the first few hours of seeing each other again after any protracted separation. She defensive, he accommodating, eventually coming together to find commonality and harmonious good humor. The process was just taking longer than usual. And events of the last few months were to blame.

She's right, he thought to himself. *If there was love in those letters, it was between the lines, not on the surface of the words themselves.* He was thinking he hated Ernest Hemingway.

"Give me your foot," he commanded, eager to be of service.

Katie willingly put her foot in Sagan's lap, and he took off her sock and began to massage her foot, working his way toward her knee and taking silent note of the scar tissue that had formed there.

"Ernest Hemingway, huh?"

"Ernest Hemingway."

"She said that?"

"She said that."

"Well, what exactly did she say?"

"Just what I said. That she thought of you as some kind of modern-day Hemingway."

"Well, what the hell does that mean?"

"How should I know? Maybe she was talking about your lifestyle."

"My lifestyle?"

"You know. Wine, women, and song?"

Katie smiled at him and he smiled back. She was teasing him, he was sure of it, and her smile was the confirmation.

He countered by squeezing her leg a little too hard. She winced, but the blood forcibly thrust from her toes up the length of her lower leg sent a flood of warmth to the rest of her body.

"So what's all this shaking about?" Sagan finally asked, never having lost sight of the single-minded trembling of her hands. Putting down her foot, he took her hands in his, covering them with his own in an attempt to calm her. Holding them meaningfully for a long moment, he looked deeply into her eyes, wondering once again if she could ever love him, and instantly hating himself for going there.

Gently, he released her hands.

She looked down at them now, waiting for the miracle.

But there had been no miracle. Instead, he'd gone back to his motel and spent the evening reflecting on his own life, something he preferred not to do except under extreme circumstances. Like when the IRS had come down on him for delinquent taxes, or when his father had passed away and left him nothing but the family cat and a four-pack of cat food.

He lay down and closed his eyes and, in the very moment his lids touched the other side, could see nothing but pink scar tissue above the knee he so loved. So, forgetting that exercise, he opened his eyes and grabbed a towel from the bathroom and headed for the outdoor pool that stretched for a city block – the one that was fed by underground springs and was said to have therapeutic powers – the one that she loved to go to.

The cashier was young and, taking stock of Sagan's baby-blue swimming trunks, made no effort to conceal her disdain. Somewhere along the line, Sagan reflected, he'd lost a generation of women.

"Six dollars!" he exclaimed, as she told him the cost of an evening drifting in the heated pool.

"Yeah, six bucks."

"What if I decide not to swim?"

"Why are you wearing swimming trunks if you're not going to swim?" It was a good question, but, given her age and her affinity for purple chewing gum, Sagan questioned her right to ask it.

"I think we might get some lightning," he said flatly.

"If there's lightning, everyone will have to leave the pool."

Precisely his point. "And my six dollars?"

"You'll get a rain check."

Sagan gave up and reached into the back of his swim trunks to pull out the six dollars he knew in the end he'd have to pay. He counted it carefully nonetheless, making sure there weren't any extra bills glued together by the sweat of his body.

"It's good for up to a year," the cashier told him as she stamped his hand with her favorite color.

"Terrific," he said, putting an end to the conversation.

Entering the pool area, Sagan scanned the pool for signs of Katie, who was nowhere to be seen. Had he really expected her to be there, to divine his own intentions and seek him out? No, but still – she was a mermaid of sorts, wasn't she? A water baby? A chicken of the sea? Why not tonight? Annoyed with the pubescent tone of his own wishful thinking, he considered leaving when, miracle of miracles, he caught sight of her stepping onto the diving board, then executing a splashless dive. He watched her, mesmerized, then belly flopped onto the water in her general direction.

"I'm swimming outside," he heard her saying, as they relaxed later on in the hot tub at the end of the pool. "It's night time. I look up and there are two moons in the sky."

"Do you have any clothes on?" he asked.

When Katie shot him a dirty look, he quickly added, "And what are you thinking when you see the two moons?"

"I'm thinking I'm home again. I'm happy." Scratching her arm, she added out of context, "Is it a good sign when your yellow fever vaccination itches?"

Sagan checked out her arm, the freshly vaccinated flesh, red and slightly swollen. "Why are you going to the Congo, anyway?" He sounded like a broken record, even to himself. "It's sheer... *lunacy*." The play on Luna's name wasn't intended, but there it was. "You know it and I know it."

But Katie wasn't going to get into it with him.

"You could have had me, you know," he said, checking out his six-pack stomach, and noting that it was beginning to look more like a two-liter.

"I thought we were talking about my dream."

As another couple joined them in the hot tub, Sagan lowered his voice. "You never wanted Mark."

"Didn't I? I'm not so sure."

"Ah."

"Ah. What does that mean – *Ah*? I'm not sure I've ever been in love with anybody, Sagan, much the less with –" She stopped herself, unsure of where she was going with the thought.

"Much the less with who – with me, you mean?"

"Don't start driving me crazy, okay? That's not what I meant."

"Why did you marry Mark if you didn't love him?"

It was a simple question, Katie reflected, for which she was never able to supply a simple answer. She had married him for a thousand reasons, all of which added up to less than a convincing argument. She'd been lonely. She'd never liked sleeping alone. She enjoyed cooking for two. She wanted a child, maybe two of them. He had beautiful eyes and was good enough in bed. She wanted to grow old with someone at her side in case, at any point, it took two people to make a whole of her. At another level, she had never let herself hope for a love that might in any way might be construed as true. In fact, she preferred to slide around the contours of the idea – the last thing she needed again in this lifetime was to feel secure in her love for another human being only to have that security torn away. She was in touch with this aspect of her psyche, even if she didn't feel empowered to change it.

"I guess I thought I would grow to love him." She re-thought this now and added, as if there were a logical flow,

"What surprises me still is how little it hurt when he left me. I mean, yeah, I was devastated, my life was completely rearranged by it. But I felt no pain. What do you think that means?"

"You could grow to love me, you know."

Katie stared at him, annoyed that he wasn't answering the question.

"They tell me I'm very loveable."

"You're my friend, Sagan. I do love you."

"Why do words so rich with meaning leave my heart so destitute?"

"Did you come here tonight just to torment me?"

"Not to torment you. No." It bothered him deeply that he never seemed to hit the target, but it didn't seem to stop him from trying again. "You used to laugh, Katie. We used to have such fun. I know things haven't been easy for you, but – well, I miss that grin of yours."

"Do you think there's something wrong with me? Really wrong, I mean?" She wasn't going to let go of the question, not while the one who knew her best was sitting right next to her. "Sometimes I wonder if it's in my power to have a real relationship."

"I don't think it's a question of whether it's in your power, but how much you're willing to pay the price. How much you're willing to run the risk."

She waited for more.

"The risk of having your peas unveiled," he supplied.

"You mean my Brussels sprouts," she said, attempting a smile – a smile that faltered and quickly gave way to silence.

"Maybe you're not in touch with your pain," Sagan offered, trying a different tack. "With the things that hurt you most."

Katie chewed on this a while, then said, "Have I always been that way?"

"Of course not. Anyway, it's nothing fatal. Nothing permanent. You've had some hard times, Katie. Hard times take their toll." Sagan was intent on giving the best possible answer he could, attempting to satisfy that part of her soul that needed comfort and encouragement. "It's hard to live with the idea that some things are outside the realm of your control. That the horrors of the world can barge into your space, knock over your house of cards. Life has a way of altering us, you know – just when we thought we had it all figured out."

After a moment, she said simply, "I wish I could just be happy," to which Sagan had no ready reply and after which a long silence fell between them.

"Okay," he finally said, switching gears. "Okay. I'm about to answer your original question, which was, *Why didn't it hurt when Mark left me?* Hear me out, all right? You never loved Mark. I'll say it even if you won't. Why you married someone you didn't love is a question for the experts; however, it could be argued that you only married him out of fear."

"Fear?"

"Fear, yes. Fear of commitment. Fear of happiness. He turned to another woman when he realized you didn't love him, which he could only have done if he didn't love you either – so hey, probably a good thing in the end. Your ego was bruised but your soul was secretly rejoicing. It was a wash, hurt and happiness merging on mutual ground. Ergo, you felt nothing at all."

Katie stared at him, apparently satisfied with the explanation. Or, at the least, hypnotized by it.

"Can we get back to the Congo now?" he ventured.

"No."

"Norwalk is a joke. You know that, right?"

"He was a great man in his day."

"*Was*, yes. Now he's a great gardener, and the Movement has been on hold for at least ten years. It's what happens when pruning sheers come too close to the face of politics."

"You're losing me."

"He's living in the past, Katie. Don't tell me you haven't noticed. The guy's stuck in the world of bulk mailings with no way out. There is no Movement. I mean that in every sense. It's been interesting, I'll give you that, but now it's out of control, and I can't sit here and watch you risk your life for absolutely nothing. I mean, what kind of friend would I be if –"

"It wasn't absolutely nothing to Muriel." Katie bristled, and Sagan quickly began to regret that he'd once again overstepped his fragile boundaries. Still, Katie knew he was right about Norwalk – about being stuck in the world of bulk mailings. There hadn't been any real progress in the Movement to speak of in a long time – though maybe, she liked to think, because the time wasn't right for it. Then again, there was the frustration of working under someone who was operating in cheerful oblivion to the technological advances of the last three decades. She knew this was true, but she felt neither empowered, nor sufficiently motivated to change it, nor was she of a mind to discuss it with Sagan, who wanted nothing more than permission to jump feet first into the heart of the matter.

"You're not a true believer, Sagan. I know that, and it's okay. Maybe I'm not either. But at least I respect the efforts of those who were. Who still are." Struck by a sudden revelation, she added, "Is that why you came to Colorado? To talk me out of going?"

Sagan was about to defend himself, to tell a white lie if he had to, when Katie suddenly rose to get out of the hot tub.

"I'm concerned about you," Sagan said with some desperation. But she was leaving now, and there was nothing for Sagan to do but call after her. "Katie, wait!"

He wasn't able to sway her though, and was left in the end to wait by the ladies' room, a short distance from the young cashier, while Katie changed her clothes. The cashier gave him the once-over, though not unkindly, and Sagan finally tendered, "It's starting to rain."

At this, the cashier tried to get a good look outside, about to debate the issue, when Katie came out of the ladies' room.

Sagan followed her outside. She talked as she walked, her mind made up, not waiting for him to catch up with her. "I can't help who I am," she said, "or who I've become. And if I don't please you, Sagan, there's nothing I can say except I'm sorry."

"You please me. What are you talking about? Of course you please me. Why do you think I – ?" He was stumbling over his own words. "Katie, for your own sake – please – don't go. To the Congo, I mean."

"I swear if you bring up that Congo thing again, I'm going to have to scream."

"I'm begging you not to be so reckless with your life. Norwalk has no right to ask this of you."

Katie found her bicycle parked against the bicycle rack.

"Haven't you been through enough?" He gave his punch line all he had.

Using flippancy as a personal shield she responded, "Duty calls!"

"Duty calls! Duty calls! That's so profound, it's what I say when I have to piss!" Katie's resolve to be annoyed softened as she watched Sagan tremble with cold in the brisk night air. It was so like him to touch her heart just when she was trying to distance herself from him. "Your lips are blue," she said, reaching up to touch them, then adding as she quickly retracted her fingers, "I have to go."

She straddled her bicycle.

"Hey...!" Sagan called out as she started to leave.

"What?"

"You're still riding it." It. The bicycle he gave her.

"Still works."

"Why don't you put a lock on it when you leave it outside?"

"Who's going to take it? It's ten years old and it looks like hell. I'll see you, okay?"

That's it? he said to himself. *I'll see you?* And then he remembered that it always ended like this, in superficial words, in feelings unspoken, in goodbyes that might preface picking up a gallon of milk at the grocery store.

Katie gave him a small smile before riding away.

"I'll paint it for you when I see you again!" he called after her.

"I'll send you a postcard!" she yelled back.

He watched her ride away, doing his best to hold on to his heart which, if it could have, would have found a place in her pocket and ridden into the sunset alongside her.

She sat at the kitchen table, looking down at the absence of her wedding ring. In the end, despite the soap and water, it hadn't been gracious enough to slide from her finger, and she'd had to forcibly pull the ring from the knuckle, ripping her skin in the process.

And yet she'd felt no pain. She thought about what Sagan had said about hurt and happiness merging on mutual ground, and decided that, despite the apparent logic of his argument, his explanation made no sense at all. It was just

Sagan exercising the fine art of bullshit, taking it to uncharted heights where it might be construed as rhetoric at its most profound. It was sweet of him, of course, but it was still bullshit. If she felt no pain, it was for one reason, and for one reason only. Because she had, quite plainly, grown numb and unfeeling. Yet, she could sense that there was still a world of feeling beneath the numbness – a place of wonder and innocence where Muriel's arms were still around her.

Muriel's passing had been a horrible blow, Samuel's coldness only adding to Katie's sense of isolation. But she had managed to free herself of Samuel's grip, and to see him for what he was – an old man, embittered by years of butting his head against the wall of an apparently unenlightened world – a man whose own darkness was compounded by the insidious effects of a growing dementia.

At the age of eighteen, having come into the modest sum of money that Muriel had left her, Katie had taken time off from college to travel the world on her own. The odyssey had been a crazy, frightening, sobering and, overall, illuminating experience, and she realized, in retrospect, that she'd been lucky to survive it intact. But it had served to convince her that her parents' lifelong struggle to create a just and peaceful world was a cause worth fighting for.

It was during this period, while she wandered aimlessly through parts of China and India, that the seriousness of Samuel's condition became obvious to those around him. Katie was reached, belatedly, but not too late.

She arrived at Samuel's deathbed to find him remarkably lucid, despite the Alzheimer's that consumed him, and able to verbally communicate with those around him. Lucidity did nothing to serve him, however. In fact, it only served to remind Katie of the insensitivity under which she had spent some of the most formative years of her life. Still, she couldn't help but feel sorry for the man who had seen fit, those many years ago, to take in the orphaned child as his own. Accordingly, she was willing to grant him the respect due to a person who, for reasons which would probably remain forever unclear to her, was tenacious enough to spend a lifetime in pursuit of an impossible dream. An impossible dream that was well beyond his own limited capacity to accomplish, and which, after Muriel's passing, he seemed to subconsciously sabotage at every step.

There were words in those final, lucid moments – he finally realizing that the baton must be handed over but, even at the edge of death, too reluctant to thrust it in her direction. She was glad for that – glad not to see the baton come her way. She had never wanted it, nor aspired to it, only dreaded the prospective weight of it. And it was only free of Samuel, free of any bondage or responsibility he might have wished to impose upon her, that she allowed herself to consider the prospect of contributing her talents to the pursuit of Muriel's noble dream. It was in her name only that she would join the battle, and not in Samuel's, a man who was too complex and too withdrawn to give her inspiration. And so it was that she had, in her own time and in her own way, tip-toed back into the world from which she had consciously distanced herself.

Looking back on the stages of her life, she could see the circular tracks, the ups and downs, of the roller-coaster ride. She noted that she had gone from wide-eyed faith and wonder in her youth to a sort of hard-earned cynicism in her teenage years, and finally back to the rudiments of faith in adulthood, though it was neither wide-eyed, nor full of wonder. It was a spark, and just a spark – the knowledge that she was surely on

Earth for a reason. This awakening happened to coincide with, and to be energized by, Samuel's passing. But that spark of mission, in and of itself, brought her no particular joy, for, just as she was getting back on her feet, life saw fit to deal her yet another blow – and, intent at some level on preserving what was left of her fragile emotions, she consciously closed the door that led to the heights and depths of feeling.

Katie went to the sink now and filled the teapot with water, then put it on the stove top to boil, a mechanical edge to her motions, as if her mind had all but departed, leaving only some primordial instinct in charge. In essence, she was disconnected from her *self* – a lizard's tail that periodically thrashed about despite being separated from its host.

Taking a seat at the table, she stared into the void of night through the open window. The rain was falling, but tonight she didn't notice.

After a while, the teapot whistled, gently at first, then obstinately.

But Katie heard no sound. The tail, as it were, had stopped moving.

- 6 -

The Way There

 *THE NIGHT SHE TOOK OFF HER* wedding ring gave way to yet another day. Katie left Colorado on a cold and dreary morning in June, a day on which there were predictions of unseasonable snow.

The sun was shining when she got on the airplane. A good omen, she told herself. A portent of good things to come. And then she remembered she didn't believe in good omens or portents of things to come. And so, she settled in for the flight to New York, not with expectation, but simply with a sense of duty and an earnest resolve to do her best.

JFK INTERNATIONAL AIRPORT – June 1, 1997

Katie made her way past the usual crowds of relatives and friends to find Sagan waiting for her, wearing a camera, a duffle bag and a shit-eating grin.

"No – don't tell me," Katie said, dropping her carry-on at his feet. "What changed your mind?" She was doing her best not to betray the fact that she was both happy and relieved to see him.

"Topeka," he said flatly, taking her carry-on. "How about a drink?"

"Not now. We'll miss our flight." Sagan was visibly disappointed and Katie found herself strangely moved by his little-boy pout. Never mind that he was pouting over alcohol. "We've got a 24-hour layover in Barcelona," she heard herself saying. "I'll buy you a beer when we get there."

Walking ahead of him, she held out her hand in anticipation of some unspoken return. By rote, Sagan reached into his pocket, then, coming up empty, turned to his other pocket, and then his duffle bag, from which he finally pulled his passport. He handed the passport to Katie, who tucked it neatly away.

They boarded the flight to Barcelona, taking designated seats rows apart from each other, he deciding he might as well have that drink before closing his eyes, and wondering why he'd come along on what he perceived to be an ill-fated journey. But the answer was obvious to him, even without the martini to clear his brain. Unable to talk her out of it, he couldn't let her go to the Congo alone.

Why Katie had chosen to continue the struggle, after all the years of discontent, all the contempt she felt for Samuel's approach to both her and the rest of humanity, was a little beyond the scope of Sagan's imagination. Hard-nosed and unrelenting, Samuel had been driven by some deep-seated need to change the world, some karmic urge, some manifest destiny. But he'd been interpersonally inept, unable to respond to people in ways that served to forward his cause. Still, Katie had come to terms with Samuel in some unspoken way and come to conclusions that she had yet to share with Sagan in full. And he had never had any choice in the matter but to simply sit back and respect her decision.

The flight to Barcelona was uneventful. Wrapping a blanket around herself, Katie decided to forego dinner to take a sleeping pill. Sagan kept a watchful eye out – though for what, he wasn't quite sure. He only knew that sleep wasn't going to come to him until he was exhausted. Or he'd had a couple more drinks. And besides, he didn't really want to sleep. Not quite yet. He found a reason to walk by the row of seats in which Katie was sitting, eager to catch a glimpse of her sleeping face. And then he sat back down and opened a magazine, only to find himself re-reading the same paragraph with no more comprehension the third time than the first. Finally, he turned out the overhead light, and tried to get some rest.

They landed on schedule and managed to clear customs in Barcelona without a hitch, their suitcases safely routed on to their ultimate destination.

That done, Sagan asked, "How about that drink?"

"You look like you spent the night on an airplane," she replied, brushing the hair from his forehead.

"With some guy's elbow in my ear. Now, about that drink..."

"Can't. Have to meet the kid."

"What kid?"

Katie glanced at her watch. "You know. The kid."

But he didn't know. She'd never told him. So he followed her, aching for the touch of her hand on his forehead again, or for that drink if nothing else, and wondering what he was going to have to do to get it.

They arrived at the gate to find that the flight had already landed. Flight 354 from Los Angeles. How could she ever forget it? The kid had hammered it into her head for eternal safe-keeping.

"What does he look like?" Sagan asked, watching the passengers come out of the customs area and into the main terminal.

"He's supposed to be looking for me. I told him I'd be wearing a yellow dress."

Sagan looked her up and down. "Why isn't she wearing a yellow dress, I wonder out loud," he finally said.

Katie conducted a quick self-check, noting she was neither in yellow, nor wearing a dress. "Shit," she said. Then to Sagan, with urgency, "Look for a young, overly enthusiastic kid with long hair. Glasses. Damn. I can't believe I didn't bring his picture."

Long hair tied behind his head and not wearing glasses, RJ Cutter came into the terminal, threw his oversized duffle bag over his shoulder, and did a quick scan of the area. He landed on Katie almost instantly and looked directly into her eyes, trying to get her attention. But she was looking right through him, intent on the other side. He smiled and made a beeline for her.

"Katie Cagle?" he said, stopping just short of her feet.

"Yes? Yes! RJ Cutter. How'd you know me?"

"You're exactly the way I pictured you. Minus the yellow dress."

"Yeah, well, I'm sorry about that."

Sagan put out a hand and RJ quickly shook it. "Hey! RJ Cutter."

"Jacques Sagan." Sagan pronounced it the French way, the way he did when he was trying to make an impression. Or simply trying to be annoying. Or both.

"Sagan," Katie said, Americanizing him against his will. "He's coming along to do some reporting for the Bulletin."

"Where's Mr. Norwalk?"

"He's not well. He'll join us in Brazzaville."

"All right! Brazzaville! Whoa! Can't believe I'm actually going!"

Well, there he is, Katie told herself, recalling the enthusiasm of his voice over the telephone. *RJ Cutter, delegate extraordinaire. In the youthful flesh.* She couldn't help but smile.

"Something funny?" RJ asked. But she ignored the question, heading instead for the terminal exit, and RJ quickly forgot the question in an attempt to keep up. "Here, let me get that," he said, taking Katie's carry-on bag.

Katie reclaimed her bag. "I can handle it," she said. Now Sagan went to take the bag from Katie, but she quickened her pace to escape him.

"What's the matter with Norwalk?" RJ asked Sagan, who now lagged casually behind.

"Had to go to the hospital," Sagan said, tapping his chest in the general area of his heart and giving a pained expression to indicate heart trouble.

"Are we talking gall bladder?" RJ asked. "Because I know a thing or two about gall bladder."

"We're talking heart."

"Heart trouble. Sure. I guess you were pointing in the wrong area."

"Well, I know a thing or two about heart," Sagan said in self-defense. "Like where it's located, for example."

RJ didn't miss the sarcasm, but he was in too good a mood to take it personally. "He's going to be okay, I hope," he said good-naturedly.

RJ chose not to pop any more questions, and instead, quickened his pace to catch up with Katie. On a parallel course now, he went to take her bag from her again. She looked into his eyes and held fast for only a moment before letting him take it. *Something about his eyes,* she told herself, wondering what it was about him she found herself liking. *Something about their shape and color and essence. Clear and pure and poignant, like Muriel's. But gentle like* ...she searched for the measure of gentle and came up with Sagan's soul.

In short-lived moments of boredom and clarity, she had wondered what Barcelona would be like. She'd been to Spain before, Madrid to be exact, but all she remembered of it was that she wasn't able to sleep at night for all the noise, and that, for some reason, she'd been on a chocolate-with-hazelnuts binge. She'd deviated from that staple to have what appeared to be some sort of French fry sandwich at the train station, only to find that the fries were part of a main body of octopus. After that, she'd quickly reverted to chocolate. Later in life, when years of travel would accustom her to a diversity of culinary oddities, she would learn to appreciate octopus in its various presentations – though never again between two pieces of bread.

She loved all the major cities of Europe. But, as she wandered the streets with Sagan and RJ, she found herself falling in love with Barcelona. The quaintness of the city, the architecture, the friendliness of the people, the nightlife. It pleased her that she was falling in love, even if it was with something as inanimate as a city. But then again, there was nothing remotely inanimate about Barcelona.

"What's that?" Katie asked as they passed a monument in the middle of one of the town squares.

"It's a monument to Christopher Columbus," RJ told her, as if it were the most self-evident of things. "Erected for the 1888 World Exposition."

Later, they looked for a place to have a drink, finally deciding on a nightclub that turned out to be smoke-filled and so loud, conversation was next to impossible. They took a table near the stage and ordered beers, pooling their Spanish coins to pay the tab.

The ear-piercing music finally stopped, to be quickly replaced by a mild-mannered guitarist. Sagan downed his beer and waved to the waiter, indicating another round for everyone.

"We've got to get up in the morning," Katie admonished.

"If we don't go to bed, we don't have to get up."

"I'm with him," RJ chimed in.

Outnumbered, Katie settled in for a long night that was now taking a frightening turn toward karaoke, headed by a drunk Japanese tourist doing an Elvis imitation at the top of his lungs.

Katie drowned him out with a second beer. Yet a third one was required when Sagan got up from the table and took the stage and the microphone. At this, Katie leaned over the table to tell RJ, "If he starts singing show tunes from the fifties, we're out of here."

Apparently needing to give life to the heartache that always seemed to plague him after a few drinks, Sagan had chosen instead a melancholy old French love song, *Plaisir d'Amour*. Katie reached for RJ's beer now and downed it as she moaned, "Here we go." But she survived the song with relative good humor, and RJ, who was enjoying the whole thing immensely, commented at the end, "Wow. That was so bad, it was good."

The night had ended in the lap of morning, Katie so dead to the world by then that she had trouble recalling the evening's events. In reconstructing the memory, she would vaguely recall the three of them on stage, singing a disco hit from the seventies, followed by the inevitable show tunes with no music to back them, and a Phil Collins song that RJ had insisted on. She would remember the audience humming and singing along appreciatively in a variety of languages and at various levels of sobriety. In his element, Sagan was virtually unstoppable. And it wasn't until the tables were emptying and Sagan was snuffing his cigarette out on the table top instead of into the ashtray two inches away, that Katie had rallied her inner troops and insisted they all get the hell out of there.

They had nosed their way to the beach, literally by smelling the salt in the air or, at least, that's the way Sagan described his methodology, which happened to work, although exactly how circuitously was anybody's guess.

Katie was eager to walk on the beach – one, to feel the sand beneath her feet and two, to wear off the effects of too much alcohol. The beach was empty, except for the three of them and a few other stragglers. Breathing deeply of the cool night air, Katie took off her shoes and began to walk, dropping one of her shoes in the process.

RJ was quick to pick it up. "So you two guys know each other pretty well?" he asked, handing Katie her shoe.

"Katie used to live in Paris back when I was a reporter for the Paris Tribune."

"That's right! Cagle lived in France in – what was it, the late sixties, early seventies?" Then, to Katie, "Hey, what was it like growing up with a major icon?"

Apparently disinterested in the conversation, Sagan had become distracted by the novelty of his surroundings and, still driven by a half-dozen dark ales that were slow to wear off, left to play tag with the Mediterranean.

Katie walked on without him, RJ at her side.

"How old are you, anyway?" she asked him.

"Twenty-three."

"College?"

"Working on my masters in political science. UCLA."

"And clearly obsessed with the idea of world government."

"I guess so. Hey, you as crazy as your dad? I've heard lots of stories."

"How can you tell?"

"How can you tell what?"

"If you're crazy."

RJ froze her in his frame of vision, then, having taken his secret measurements, opted to ignore the question. "I wanted to tell you, I'm really sorry about – what was her name? Luna? You've got guts to keep on going. I really admire you for that."

But she didn't feel admirable in the least. She let herself think of Luna for the briefest moment before pushing her out of her mind again.

"Pour la jolie demoiselle," Sagan said, running up to them with a handful of seashells and extending his hand to Katie in offering. *For the pretty young lady.*

Katie stared at Sagan's outstretched hand, not meaning to be unkind, just slow to respond.

In the meantime, RJ took a seashell from Sagan's hand and examined it with genuine interest. "Awesome," he commented.

Sagan dropped the seashells with little fanfare and suggested a swim. "What do you say?"

"I say I'm not that drunk," Katie answered. "But if you are, go right ahead."

But before Sagan could take a step in that direction, RJ was already well on his way into the ocean, fully clothed. He yelled as he hit the cold water – a primeval yell, a yell that told the world that RJ Cutter was alive and about to make his splash. Sagan, just as vocal, quickly followed.

Katie watched them, smiling at their in-the-moment joie de vivre. Was it beginning to rub off on her? She took a seat to wait for them, contemplating the sand as she sifted it through her fingers. Now she turned her gaze to the sky, where the moon was just coming out from behind a cloud. And there it was again. That feeling she got on certain nights when the moon was too blue. That nameless longing, that aching hole in her heart. But Sagan and RJ were on their way back to her before melancholy had a chance to consume her.

Cold and shivering, Sagan and RJ ran up the beach toward Katie, RJ uttering a string of long-winded *shits*.

"Maybe Katie will lend us her sweater," Sagan said to RJ, standing in front of Katie and shaking uncontrollably.

When Katie didn't react, Sagan knelt next to her and found tears running down her face. "Qu'est-ce qu'il y a, Katie?" he asked, solicitously. "What's going on?"

Without a word, Katie took off her sweater and dried off Sagan's face and torso, then invited RJ into the warmth of her sweater and dried him down as well. The moisture wiped from their bodies, they quietly took a seat on either side of her, waiting for her to explain herself.

"You'll both get pneumonia and die," she finally said.

"She makes predictions," Sagan explained to RJ. "They never come true."

"Why is she crying?" RJ asked. Then to Katie, realizing he might as well go straight to the source, "Why are you crying?"

"Beer makes her crazy," Sagan said, doing the talking for her. "And, well, you know, life hasn't been much fun lately either."

Katie dried her tears with the back of her trembling hands and, unsure of what to do, RJ put a hand on hers to calm her.

Staring at RJ's hand on hers, Katie stopped crying and looked up at him, searching for something of significance. His eyes met hers and he smiled at her, a pure and youthful smile that seemed to contain all the pieces of herself she longed so much to reclaim. Then he released her hand and she noticed, to her great amazement, that her hand had stopped shaking.

Wearing khaki shorts and looking like hell warmed over, Katie came down the crowded aisle of the airplane that would take them on the final leg of their journey. She found her seat only to discover RJ already seated at the window, engrossed in a book on international law.

"I think you're in my seat," Katie told him. "But keep it. I like the aisle seat better."

"Hey there. Still feeling sick?"

She was, but she didn't want to talk about it. Bad enough that they'd been obliged to watch her vomit in the street on the way back to the hotel.

RJ put down his book. "I'm thinking maybe we should change a little money at the airport to get us by. Then maybe we can hit a bank in Brazzaville. Get a better exchange rate."

Katie didn't bother with a response but, instead, put her carry-on in the overhead compartment and sat down. She fastened her seat belt and gave it a solid tug, propelling a wave of nausea toward her throat. No, not a wave. A tsunami. Putting that feeling aside, she scanned the airplane for the nearest exit.

"Six rows up," RJ informed her. "On the left. Don't worry. I've got it all scoped out."

"How could I be worried with an immortal 23-year-old in the seat next to me?"

"In a bad mood?"

"Lack of sleep makes me hateful. Where's Sagan?"

Katie looked around and found Sagan a couple of rows back, staring straight at her. He waved and she waved back before turning around and settling into her seat.

"If anybody on this plane is immortal," RJ observed, "I think it might be him."

Katie closed her eyes, and RJ checked her out for a brief moment, finally determining that whatever conversation there might have been had now ended. In his young world, where there was always tomorrow, the end of a conversation was nothing to be mourned. He picked up his book and resumed his reading.

Sagan walked down the aisle, on his way back from the bathroom. Except for a handful of other die-hards, the plane was sleeping now. He nodded at RJ who was – Sagan couldn't tell – either wide awake and just zoned out, or sleeping with his eyes open, a skill that Sagan himself had once taken pride in mastering as a young student.

He took his seat and wondered if there was a chance of getting a Bloody Mary. *And they're off to the Congo!* he heard his mind saying in that contemptuous tone of voice he reserved for moments of self-recrimination. It's just that he wasn't into mindless martyrdom and, in his mind, that was just what he had gotten himself into. Granted, he couldn't have let her do it by herself but, even so, it grated at him that they were compromising their lives for nothing. It didn't take a sage or a psychic to know that all hell was going to break loose again in the Congo at some point. He could only pray it wouldn't be while they were there. Pray and have a Bloody

Mary. Where was that flight attendant, anyway? And why was she shirking her God-given responsibilities?

The nonsense of meeting in the Congo notwithstanding, he had no great objections to the cause. But he'd seen the face of suffering enough to know he'd rather be in Topeka, planting corn in that piece of weed-infested turf he called a backyard. He'd seen enough of death and dying to know he'd rather be alive. He turned on his call button and prayed to the gods of beverage service for a rapid response.

Unlike Sagan, RJ didn't know a thing about sleeping with his eyes open. Once he configured his mind for sleep, he was out. And when he woke up, he was up. It was really that simple. Right now he was up and restless with anticipation. He opened his window shade slightly and peeked out over a darkened sky. Closing it again, he fixed his gaze straight ahead, turning his thoughts to the multitude of youthful preoccupations that constantly played in his head.

His girlfriend, for one. The one he was crazy about, who was, as far as he could tell, crazy about him. He wasn't sure what to make of it, though. He'd been crazy about others and, in the end, it'd always been short-lived. *The only constant is change itself*, he told himself, constructing a good case for avoiding an early marriage. And yet, he missed her and longed for her. Still, he had this singular facility for putting her out of his head, and here and now he exercised the option in favor of other concerns.

That student loan, for example. The one he had used to pay for his trip to the Congo. No use relying on his parents for anything there. They didn't have it. And besides, his father wouldn't have approved. Hated politics. Hated politicians too.

"No reason I can't be an honest one," RJ had told his father, defending his own cause and simultaneously wondering if he himself would be subject to defilement. But he didn't give the thought more than a moment to cavort in his mind before pushing it outside the cerebral wall. He'd be a great politician, end of story. He'd be more than a representative of the people – he'd be an integral part of orchestrating the plans for a better world.

To RJ, the choice was pretty simple: global unity or global annihilation. Nuclear war or nuclear disarmament. Environmental destruction or environmental sustainability. The idea of a Federation of Earth under a constitution was no more absurd in his view than the idea of a constitutional United States of America. After all, the Founding Fathers had not set out, in 1787, to diminish the jurisdiction or power of states, but to create a structure under which the risk of interstate conflict could be minimized, and the common good of all sustained. And, with today's critical concerns extending far beyond the boundaries of nations, it was, in RJ's estimation, time to go back to the drawing board. But why re-invent the wheel? The basic blueprint was there, just waiting for the world to get it together – to finally face the needs of a planet spinning out of control.

There was no doubt in RJ's mind that the ideology of the rule of sovereign nations was hopelessly outdated – obsolete, in fact – and things would have to change if humanity was going to survive.

But right now he was hungry and he needed a breakfast bar. He looked in his pocket as if expecting to find one there. *It's happened before*, he told himself, fully believing in minor miracles, but still coming up empty.

If Katie was sleeping at all, it was the sleep of the vigilant. And now, with RJ's stirring, she awakened, her eyes landing on his young and hopeful face. *A true-believer,* she told herself, conscious of a faint underlying sarcasm. A true-believer with a strangely compelling personality and a face she found herself studying, as if to decipher its hidden agendas.

Not unaware that he was being scrutinized, RJ looked her way. He smiled at her – a smile she didn't return.

"I thought you wore glasses," she said.

"Not anymore. Contacts."

It was only a seed of conversation but, for unknown reasons, it gave rise to buried emotions. She found herself drifting into the land of unspoken thoughts, of long-forgotten dreams and regrets. Was it lack of sleep? Against her will, she gave them life.

"I think betrayal is the greatest evil of all. What do you think?"

"Whoa. I'm not sure. What are we talking about?"

"Do you have a girlfriend, Mr. Cutter?"

"You threw up on my foot last night. I think you can call me RJ. And yes, I do."

"What's she like?"

"I'm afraid I'm a little prejudiced. How about you? Got a husband? Boyfriend?"

"A husband. Once upon a time. Not anymore. Kind of like your glasses, but with no contacts to replace them."

"Any children?" he asked after mulling that one over. And there he was, pressing his finger against the most painful place in her psyche.

"Last night you asked about my father," she said. "Are you really interested?"

"Yeah, of course. Totally."

"A lot of people thought my father was crazy."

"Well, was he, or wasn't he?"

"His whole life had only one focus. You tell me. Is that what it is to be crazy?"

"In retrospect, we like to call that genius."

In fact, RJ was right. Despite his failings as a human being, Samuel had been a genius. A voracious reader with a photographic memory and a mind like a sponge. More than that, he had been able to do what others couldn't – integrate the facts, see the total picture, intellectually apply them to a distant future.

"I wondered for the longest time – you know, after he died and I had time to dwell on it and pick it all apart – how he must have felt at that final moment, knowing that all he had ever worked for was nowhere near becoming a reality." In fact, she had often wondered if Samuel had fallen into hell. But why was she telling RJ all this?

"And?" RJ nudged her on.

"I don't think you want to hear this."

"I do. Really. Swear."

"I guess none of us knows what that last moment will be like, do we?"

"I've read a little about near-death experiences. The other side isn't such a bad place, from what I can gather. But the common denominator still seems to be that everyone's pretty happy they didn't cross over." And then he added, realizing he was probably missing the point. "But that's not what you're getting at, is it?"

"Something tells me that what you experience at the moment of death has something to do with the way you live your life. And if that's the case, then I think – well, I think my mother may have experienced the most profound joy."

"Okay. And what about your father?" RJ was as eager to know the scoop on Samuel Cagle as Katie was reluctant to talk about him.

"I think it was only faith in some greater purpose, some greater tomorrow, that allowed her to put such unrelenting effort into the void, into all the apparent nothingness. Do you understand what I mean?"

"I'm not sure. Maybe. I think so."

Looking into RJ's eyes, she found herself obligated to answer the question still hanging between them. "I was never close to my father," she offered. "I know you'd like to know more about him, but believe me, I'm not the one to talk to."

RJ left it at that and Katie was grateful. She was never eager to talk about Samuel, afraid that scratching the surface of her past would give way to a torrent of ill-feelings that she would later regret having expressed.

Katie studied her naked ring finger before continuing, not sure where she was headed, but pretty certain she wasn't going to stop until she got there.

"I was married almost five years before I got pregnant," she found herself saying.

RJ mulled this over, not sure of the relevance, and feeling vaguely uncomfortable in the unfamiliar territory.

"I labored for twenty-one hours knowing the baby was dead."

RJ felt himself both recoiling at the subject matter and being sucked into the growing vortex. He wasn't going to nudge for more this time, but he wasn't going to try and stop her from elaborating either.

"When my water broke,'' she finally continued, "I remember thinking, *This kid's going to be a basketball player* – he was so active. Turns out the umbilical cord was wrapped around his neck."

Even now, the memory was strangely muted. Labor had been hell. Contractions one on top of the other from the start. Unbearable pain that gave way to worse, followed by an anti-climatic birth and a dreamlike aura of detachment – a detachment that had come too late and manifested itself only in a strangely tranquil post-partum depression. There had been physical pain, emotional pain, and mental pain, and they had rolled into one overwhelming agony and conquered her.

"Next morning, the nurse said, *Not very busy in there*, and I said, *You should have been there last night!* Of course, they couldn't get a heartbeat. The baby was dead and I had to go on with the whole thing as if it were still alive. As if there were still joy at the end of all the pain."

After a long interval, in which RJ searched his brain for something remotely appropriate to say, he finally ventured, "Was it a boy or a girl?" instantly reproaching himself for having asked.

Gratefully, Katie ignored the question, finishing the stream of thought instead. "After the birth – the death – I came to understand my mother's heart "

"And now you share her vision?"

"No. Not her vision. Like I said. Her heart."

RJ wasn't oblivious to the fact that Katie had again managed to maneuver the conversation back to her mother. He figured she had her reasons, though he was a little uncomfortable with her implied indifference to Samuel, one of his personal heroes. Then again, heroes were made to be toppled. He knew that, and, always of a mind to question the fabric of heroism, he was okay with it.

They talked a while longer, mostly her – she was vaguely aware of it – and somewhere in the conversation, she found sleep and, ultimately, the warmth of RJ's shoulder. No longer vigilant, she succumbed to the sweet repose of the weary mind that had found its way to harbor.

The Congo

MAYA MAYA INTERNATIONAL AIRPORT
JUNE 3, 1997

 *ESTABLISHED SOMEWHERE IN THE Fourth Century, the Congo was originally composed of three primal kingdoms – the Loango, the Teke, and the Kongo. In 1910, the Middle Congo became part of French Equatorial Africa. Reforms, inaugurated under Charles de Gaulle and the French Constitution of 1946, conferred French citizenship upon the Congolese. On April 15, 1960, the People's Republic of the Congo became an independent nation.*

Located near the Equator in west central Africa, the Congo extends 1,280 kilometers inland from the Atlantic Ocean...

Light was pouring in through half-opened window shades as the flight attendant announced, "Ladies and gentlemen, the pilot has turned on the seat belt sign in preparation for our landing in Brazzaville." She would repeat it in a couple of other languages, French and Lingala, as far as Sagan could tell over the static and the baggage-rattling turbulence. He put down the pamphlet he was reading – *The People's Republic of the Congo: Facts You'll Want to Know* – and sipped his tomato juice – the bloody without the Mary – as he looked out the window at the world below with growing apprehension.

Up a few rows and wide awake, RJ stared out his own window with unabashed youthful wonder. Katie leaned over him to get a glimpse out the window, not unaffected by his enthusiasm.

"The Congo River," he said in reference to the river that could now be seen snaking its way between the cities of Brazzaville and Kinshasa.

Looking out the window, her head next to his, their smiles, like the smiles of innocent children, converged into one.

It was hot when they got off the plane, but not quite as suffocating as the plane itself which, somewhere along the line, had lost all of its ventilation. Sagan's back was soaked with sweat as he headed for the tarmac behind Katie and RJ. Conducting a personal inventory, from the vacuum in his ears to the stiffness in his knees, he came to the conclusion that he was feeling uncomfortable in just about every possible human way.

Katie headed for a small contingency of Congolese, dressed in local costumes, who had apparently gathered there to greet them, as evidenced by their make-shift sign that read simply, *Federation of Earth.*

I'm not sure I'd brag about it, Sagan was thinking as he took stock of the handful of people that constituted the welcoming committee. But then he took a deep breath and tried to right his attitude.

"Je suis Mademoiselle Katie Cagle des États Unis," Katie said, introducing herself, then introducing Sagan and RJ.

The excitement of having visitors from the United States was evident in the smiling faces of the greeters, who eagerly shook everyone's hands. First in line was Bernard Biyoudi who quickly stepped forward to identify himself as the group's leader. Katie made an attempt to mentally match the face with the small photograph he had sent in with his delegate registration application. A passionate man with an explosive laugh and soulful eyes, his skin was an ebony to rival midnight. "Tout l'monde parle français?" he asked, wanting to know if RJ and Sagan spoke French. Katie explained that Sagan did, but that RJ, unfortunately, did not.

"You don't speak French?" Biyoudi asked RJ in English.

"Afraid not," RJ said, vaguely contrite.

"I will teach you, okay?"

"Okay."

Biyoudi laughed, sending the rest of the committee, none of whom spoke English, into fits of joyful laughter.

If they think that one's funny, wait till I tell them the one about the one-eyed bullfrog, Sagan was thinking as he prepared to take the lens off his camera and asked, "J'peux prendre une photo?"

But with a sweep of his hand, Biyoudi quickly nixed the whole idea of taking photographs, explaining that the airport was a high security area and, therefore, no photographs were allowed. "Why don't you wait until we get into Brazzaville?" he suggested, cautioning him that even then, he would want to be careful.

"Don't we have to clear customs or something?" RJ asked Katie as they made their way toward the terminal.

"Please don't worry about customs," Biyoudi told him, overhearing. "For you, it's nothing. Nothing. I shall take you through myself." Biyoudi was eager to prove himself, and they followed, trying to keep pace with Biyoudi's stride, with his long legs that were eager to get to where he was going.

Meanwhile, Sagan was still itching to take photographs, but not about to, in view of the warning. He'd had enough experience to know that, given the sensitive political atmosphere, and the armed guards not so inconspicuously stationed around the airport, it wouldn't take much to set things off. "Katie," he said in her ear, diverting her attention from her host, "do you still have my passport?"

Katie gave him a familiar look – a look that said, *stop asking stupid questions.*

It's not a stupid question, Sagan was thinking, *but not a serious one either*. He caught up with Biyoudi and began to shoot the breeze in his native language which, interestingly, was a little rusty from dis-use.

"What are you doing with his passport?" RJ lagged behind to ask Katie.

"He's kind of scattered," Katie told him. "Would you have ever guessed it? How about you? You don't need a mother, do you?"

"I don't think so," he answered, then jump-skipped to another subject. "How do you say *I've never been so hot in all my goddamn life in Lingala?*"

"Ask Sagan."

"He speaks Lingala?"

"No, but he'll have an answer for you. He'll say, *you've obviously never been to Topeka in July.*"

RJ smiled. Took it in. Took in the airport. The guards. The colors. The Congo. He liked it here. It was hot, but it was raw and animated. He liked the way it made him feel – in a word, *alive* – in two words, *fully conscious* – and he decided it might be useful to memorize the moment, which he did. That done, he moved ahead to catch up with Sagan.

"Hey, Sagan!" he said, interrupting a lively conversation with Biyoudi. "How do you say, *I've never been so hot in all my goddamn life* in Lingala?"

"You're not from the Midwest, are you?" Sagan answered with some annoyance. "Topeka in August. Now that's what I call hot."

Biyoudi had always been a man of God. Which meant nothing more than that he worshiped goodness and believed that righteousness would somehow prevail. He'd been a child of privilege, his junior year spent at Georgetown University in D.C., his senior year at Oxford.

Since his youth, he had cherished the wish to be a big man – a big man in the most meaningful sense of the words. A man whom others could look up to. A man who would do big things. After college, he came back to Brazzaville, full of dreams and youthful vitality, determined to help pull his village out of what he perceived to be the Dark Ages of the African Continent – or the dark before the dawn, as he liked to think. He had high ideals and even bigger ideas. He would put his engineering skills to work and offer his expertise to a city that was hopelessly behind the times. He would help build roads, pathways to communications. He would create job opportunities and provide fair wages – a task he worked at for years, financially supported by his wealthy and generous wife and largely undaunted by his lack of success. The birth of his daughter fueled both his resolve and his sense of futility for, in the Congo, as he would finally come to understand, the conflict, the factions, the uncertainty of day-to-day living, made it difficult to create lasting change, or gain any real footing. Rather than reach higher, he realized, he would have to dig deeper. He would have to uproot the underlying problems and then, facing them head-on, find a way to resolve them.

It wasn't long after this awakening that he met a man on the train to Pointe Noir – a man from the neighboring country of Burkina Faso, who talked to him about a movement that was beginning to emerge in various parts of Africa and whose tentacles reached, according to him, to every part of the world.

Biyoudi was immediately intrigued. "What sort of movement is this?" he wanted to know.

"It's called the Movement for the Federation of Earth," he was informed.

"And how will this Federation operate?" Biyoudi wanted to know.

"By way of a constitution."

"A constitution? What kind of constitution?" Biyoudi's interest was growing by the second.

"It will be a charter for peace."

A charter for peace. It had a nice ring.

"Yes, and then what "

"And then there will be no more strife," concluded his friend. "What will there be to fight about when all our needs are met? When there is food on the table and jobs for everyone? When no man can take away our freedom or steal our property?"

It was obvious to Biyoudi that his friend was, at the least, hopelessly naive, and at best, only superficially informed. It was obvious that there had to be a great deal more to the concept of such a worldwide movement. And Biyoudi would make it a point to find out. He thanked his friend and parted ways with him, then quickly wrote away for information. Colorado. It sounded like another world. And two months later, much to his surprise, he received a shipment containing large amounts of documentation, every word of which he read and re-read and absorbed and which became an integral part of his dreams. To his amazement, it all made sense – a federation that would bring the world together with the aim of resolving conflicts peacefully and equitably for all. A kind of United Nations, not under the influence of a few powerful countries. A United Nations legislatively empowered to do the job of maintaining the global commons, of assuring peace and prosperity for all.

Biyoudi was a man of God. And to him, this was the work of a true disciple. Within six weeks, he had established a chapter in Brazzaville, and within six months, the chapter could brag of over 75 members. For this idea of a world under one universal flag had put a fire in his soul.

Customs hadn't exactly been the breeze that Biyoudi had predicted. RJ – probably due to his long hair and slightly inappropriate nonchalance – got hassled and subjected to a fairly in-depth baggage search, which ended with Biyoudi making a lot of noise on the sidelines while RJ emptied his pants pockets, only to lay a scrunched breakfast bar out for public viewing and politically-motivated dissection.

"I wondered where it went," he later told Katie.

She smiled, thinking back on this as she put down her suitcase, closed the door behind her, and set about checking out her hotel room. Twin beds, clean, modern. Nice, were it not for the armored beetle in the corner and the implications of the mosquito netting above the bed.

She was bone-tired from the whole journey, though less from the flight than from the drive through the streets of Brazzaville. Biyoudi had brought a small caravan to the airport, a few old camouflage Jeeps, and his own personal vehicle – an antiquated Citroën. Katie had spent the entire drive staring out the window at Brazzaville, largely ignoring Biyoudi's excited and essentially one-way conversation – Brazzaville in all its beauty, squalor and mayhem. Here, a woman pounding plantain – there, merchants peddling goods.

Children's laughter resonating over the horrors of poor sanitation, malnutrition and disease, streets crowded to capacity against the backdrop of occasionally modern buildings, and armed soldiers sporadically and strategically situated. One of the soldiers had stared back at Katie as they drove past and, mesmerized, she had remained glued to his eyes until she could no longer turn her head far enough to remain connected.

But now she was at the hotel – the best that Brazzaville had to offer, and not bad by any standards. She was tired, her mind over-stimulated, her body weak and exhausted.

She went to the bathroom and turned on the light. Modern enough. She flushed the toilet. No problem there. She turned on the water, which gushed out clear. She noted the sign on the wall above the sink in French and someone's version of the Queen's English: *Eau non-potable. Please don't drink of the water.*

Leaving the bathroom, she opened the sliding glass door and stepped outside onto her private veranda where a light rain was falling – just enough to soften her skin without saturating it. She rubbed the moisture into her arms, the gesture reminiscent of the tenderness of a father she once knew. She was three floors up, and separated by half-walls from other verandas, none of which were currently occupied. Looking down at the unused tennis courts and beyond that, at the town of Brazzaville, she realized in a surge of emotion that might best be described as panic, that she was actually there.

RJ walked out onto his own veranda now, the one next to hers, and they exchanged nods, quickly returning their gazes to Brazzaville.

"Is that the river?" Katie asked after a moment.

He was hoping she would ask. "The Congo river. Second only to the Amazon in sheer volume."

"What are you – some kind of walking Chamber of Commerce?"

"Nah, I just like to read up on stuff. Especially if it's going to have a major bearing on my life."

"What makes you think this trip is going to have a major bearing on your life?" Katie herself fell easily into visions of catastrophe, though she seldom allowed herself to really think about it.

"I've never been outside the U.S. before. And, obviously, I've never been to a – well, you know, to a constitutional convention. Anyway you look at it, it's major."

"Is that Kinshasa across the way?"

RJ nodded.

"Looks bigger than Brazzaville."

"Yeah, by a long shot. Much higher crime rate too."

Down below, a Congolese boy on a bicycle smiled and waved up at them, ringing his bicycle bell as he went by. "Ey, Mondele!" he shouted.

"What'd he say?" Katie asked RJ.

"Mondele."

"What does that mean?"

"White man."

"Where'd you learn Lingala?"

"I only know a couple words. I'm working on food items at the moment. *Nsusu.* Know what that means?"

"Not a clue."

Katie leaned against the half-wall, breathing Brazzaville into her lungs.

"Don't look now," RJ informed her, "but there's a mosquito about to land on your arm."

"Nsusu means, *Don't look now, but there's a mosquito ab* – ?"

Katie was slow on the uptake, and RJ reached over the wall and slapped her arm, annihilating the enemy in the process.

"You might want to be careful," he told her. "The mosquitoes that carry Dengue Fever are urbanites. They tend to be active during the day."

Katie shrugged, wiped the blood from her arm.

"Trust me, you really don't want Dengue Fever. I know someone who came back from Zambia with a bad case. Took his doctors two months to diagnose it, and by that time he was about to lose his mind. Worse thing is, there's no cure. I'll lend you my insect repellant."

RJ headed back into his room for the repellent, coming back out in less than a flash. He hopped over the wall onto Katie's veranda and held the repellent out for her. When she didn't immediately take it, he squirted a hefty amount onto the palm of his hand and began to spread it on the arm that was almost mosquito dinner.

Katie watched him with hypnotic interest, more fascinated by his technique than in touch with the feel of his hands on her body. She volunteered, "Mosquitoes have always loved me."

"Go figure," he said, spreading the ointment over the exposed areas of her body, ending by gently applying it to the contours of her face. That done, he handed her the rest of the bottle. "There's more where this came from," he said.

Katie took the bottle, a little too uncertain to be grateful. "I'm sure there is," she said.

It was raining harder now and, in short order, it was monsoon season. They looked at each other and laughed – some kind of primal reaction to being drenched without fair warning. Katie opened her mouth to capture the rain, choking on it in the process. "I thought this was the dry season!"

But RJ wasn't laughing. "Hey, what are you doing?" he exclaimed. "Don't *drink* it!"

Instinctively, Katie closed her mouth.

"There's all kinds of shit in the water here. Even the rain water. You could get parasites. Or who the hell knows what. Bottled water – that's the ticket, okay?"

Katie nodded. She looked at RJ as the rain soaked her skin – looked at him and into him and beyond him. Her look was penetrating and RJ stared back uncertainly, finally relinquishing a small, but enigmatic smile.

The rain was short-lived and RJ chose to stay out on the veranda after Katie had left. On a mission to memorize a few more life moments – to mentally catalogue them even – he gazed out at his new dominion. He was amazed that he was actually there, that he had managed to translate his school loan into, not just a semester of school, but a trip to the heart of Africa. Yeah, he was broke, and he'd have to rely on the good will of others and the nourishment of that box of breakfast bars he'd brought along for good measure. But he was here, wasn't he? Hell yeah, he was!

He hadn't bothered to tell his parents about the trip, figuring they would only need to know if he happened to die on foreign soil, in which case, he wouldn't be around to regret not telling them. Anyway, had they known, they would have threatened to cut him off entirely, something he wasn't quite prepared to deal with. And anyway, he didn't want to rock the boat any more than he had to. So he'd simply told them he was going to D.C. to do some school-related research. They'd bought it enough to grumble out loud about his chosen career path, and how he ought to have had the good sense to study veterinary medicine like his brother, or refrigerator repair like his father. They'd bought it enough to sermonize that, never mind how high his ideals, politics was a contemptible profession and that, furthermore, if the world could be changed for the better, it wouldn't be in the shape it's in today. They'd bought it enough to wave goodbye and buy him a box of breakfast bars for the trip. The variety box, no less. For which he would be eternally grateful.

No denying it. They were coarse and rigid and unintentionally funny. And he couldn't wait to break the mold. But even so, he loved them. It's just the way it was.

RJ left the veranda now and went into his room and – not the least bit tired – deliberated between a breakfast bar and brushing his grungy teeth. It was a thing with him – clean teeth – and he decided to go for it. He turned on the bathroom light and found, in his nest of carefully laid out bathroom items, his handy foldable toothbrush. Unfolding it as if it were a secret weapon, he neatly layered on the toothpaste, then turned on the water, dipped his toothbrush under it, and began brushing his teeth. He did a thorough job of it, then rinsed off his toothbrush, folded it away, looked around for a glass, couldn't find one, cupped his hands under the faucet and took in the water that way. He gargled for a moment before halting the process mid-gargle, suddenly realizing what he'd done. Urgently spitting out the water, he grabbed his nearby mouthwash, rinsed his mouth out with that, dried his face, revisited the sign above the sink telling him not to drink the water, and looked at himself in the mirror as if he were the world's biggest loser.

"Fuck!" he saw himself say.

In his own hotel room, down the hall from RJ, Sagan smoked a cigarette, flicking the ashes into the cup of his hand as he stared out the window at a convoy of armored vehicles driving past the hotel. He took it all in, but didn't jump to conclusions, simply logged the information. He wet his fingers now and, pinching the life out of the tip of his cigarette, put the butt in his shirt pocket for future reference, and stepped away from the window. She'd had enough time to rest up and get ready, he figured.

When Katie had gone back into her room from the veranda, she was dripping wet. She dried herself off, then lay down on the bed, fell asleep, and dreamed she was a mother again. It was a beautiful baby, a boy – alive and well – and she put it to her breast with an intense longing to nurse it. But her breasts were dry and there was no milk. She had awakened from the dream feeling vaguely depressed, and made herself get up and wash her face in the hopes of shaking the feeling.

The knock on Katie's door found her with her arms stuck halfway into the armholes of that deceptively simple yellow dress she'd neglected to wear on the plane, and it took her a moment to answer. When she finally did, she found Sagan standing there.

"I think it'd be wise for us to register with the American Embassy," he said, taking in the dress, the scoop of the neck revealing just the hint of cleavage. "Need a zip?" he asked, trying his luck.

"Norwalk advised us against registering with the Embassy. The U.S. isn't exactly behind our cause, you know."

What Sagan knew was that, wherever the truth lay, Norwalk had inherited Samuel's paranoia of the CIA and had managed to pass the virus down to Katie. But Sagan wasn't about to get into it with her.

Katie decided she could use a zip, and turned around to make it easy for him.

"As an American citizen," he said, zipping up her dress and trying not to think about the curve of her back under his hands, "you're still entitled to your country's protection."

"I know that, Sagan, I just don't want to invite trouble, that's all."

"Okay. Well, then, how about registering with the U.N. Mission?"

"Are you worried?" she asked, turning around again.

He hesitated a moment before avoiding the answer. "Think about it, okay?"

"I don't think I'm going to change my mind," she said, closing the door.

She stood facing the closed door, knowing full well he was still standing on the other side of it, feeling thwarted and unfinished. She knew he was right to be concerned and, at some level, it comforted her to know he was worried on her behalf. On the other hand, she didn't want to hear the words of worry, or see the troubled face, or be reminded of the reality that she was trying so hard to ignore. She felt Sagan turn away now, knew he was walking back down the hallway, suppressing his feelings, the way she always made him do. It hurt her, and she wished things could be different.

She went back to getting dressed, to putting on her eye shadow and selecting from the three sets of earrings laid out on the vanity. The transformation complete, she studied herself in the mirror – studied the dark olive of her skin, the chisel of her cheek bones and the hazel of her eyes, the cleavage of her breasts. But the total picture was sterile to her, and she turned away.

She'd be kinder next time, she told herself.

She wondered why she'd even bothered with the hairbrush, the humidity and the drive in Biyoudi's Jeep having essentially destroyed all vestiges of style from her hair and, as they pulled up to the persimmon-colored house, surrounded by flowers and trees, Katie was too busy running her fingers through the unruliness to exclaim out loud her first reaction: *How utterly charming!*

Even by Western standards, it was a very nice house – warm, colorful, roomy yet cozy, and with ample room for entertaining.

"Lovely!" Katie finally exclaimed as she stepped in the front door.

"Simone!" Biyoudi called out.

Simone, Biyoudi's wife, hurried in from another part of the house, wearing a colorful wraparound dress and looking the height of graciousness and femininity.

"Bonsoir! Bonsoir!" she said, with the kind of enormous smile only the most generous hearts can bestow. "Welcome to our home!" She greeted them first in Lingala, and then in French. "Soyez les bien-venus!"

Sagan and Katie responded in unison. "Merci!"

"Merci!" RJ chimed in, his attempt at a French accent as grating to Sagan's ears as fingernails on a chalkboard.

But Simone took an instant liking to him and, after a few minutes of group small talk, she took his arm and escorted him to the dining room, where a five-star feast had already been laid out, complete with fine china and gold-rimmed wine glasses. She watched for his reaction as he did a visual audit of the heaping dishes of steamed vegetables and rice, onions and fried fish, breads, manioc root, and condiments. *Good bread, good meat, good God, let's eat,* he thought to himself, flashing back to the Thanksgivings of his childhood.

"Est-ce que tu as faim?" Simone asked him.

"What'd she say?" RJ asked Katie. Then to Simone, apologetically, "I'm sorry. I don't understand."

"She wants to know if you're hungry," Katie supplied.

"Yeah, starving."

No need for a translation, Simone got the picture.

Now Biyoudi's pretty eighteen-year-old daughter, Danielle, shyly entered the room, and Biyoudi introduced her to everyone present, with an emphasis on her perceived counterpart for the evening – the unsuspecting RJ.

Maneuvering RJ to sit next to Danielle, Biyoudi took his own seat at the head of the table, then went to move the profusion of flowers blocking the view of his dinner guests, his wife quick to assist.

"Mangeons!" he then said, translating for RJ. "Let us eat!" Grabbing a bottle of the wine that would continue to flow throughout the meal, he began to pour.

"So what do you think of our country, Mr. Sagan?" Biyoudi asked, eager to get the conversation going.

"Haven't seen much of it yet. Ask me again in a week."

Biyoudi began passing dishes around the table in what threatened to be an endless cycle.

"What a wonderful wine!" Katie interjected in a conscious effort to steer the subject into the trivial. There was no doubt in her mind that tonight would be one of the last nights to unwind, to enjoy the pleasures of wine and food and frivolity before meeting the challenges that lay ahead.

"Tastes a lot like a little California Chablis I know," RJ ruminated out loud.

"You like it?" Biyoudi seemed pleased.

Letting his expression do the talking, RJ smiled approvingly. "Is this manioc?" he asked, forking away at some apparently edible mass on his dinner plate.

"Yes," Biyoudi told him, impressed. "You like?"

RJ managed a vague nod of the head, but confided to Katie in an aside, "It's full of cyanide. Well, I mean they squeeze it all out before they cook it, but when it comes to cyanide, you can never be too certain."

Katie listened, instinctively nudging her manioc to one side.

"Tell me, Mr. Biyoudi," Sagan said, eager to get back to essentials, "what is the refugee situation in Brazzaville? Are they all going back to Zaire now?"

"Oh, yes, yes. Many are going back now. It was, for a while, a very bad situation. You see, there are forty million Zairians and only two and a half million Congolese. So, of course, we were very worried about the numbers coming into our country – into Brazzaville, in particular."

"Don't people need a visa or something to get from one country to the other?" Katie asked, resigning herself to the topic.

"The problem is, Miss Katie, the border between Zaire and the Congo is nearly 1,700 kilometers long," Biyoudi answered.

"The Congo River, you mean," RJ clarified.

"Yes, the river. Of course, the Congolese authorities have suspended transport between Brazzaville and Kinshasa. But where there are no ports, a boat can always cross."

"What happens to all the refugees once they get here?" Katie wanted to know.

"They are taken in by families, or they simply sleep on the street, in the markets, wherever they can. They try to survive until they feel it is safe to go home."

Simone addressed Sagan, sitting next to her, in the French they both understood. "Mr. Biyoudi tells me you are expecting more than a thousand delegates to the conference."

Sagan responded as philosophically as possible, "On verra, n'est-ce pas?" *We'll see.*

"And when will they be arriving?"

A logical question, which Biyoudi promptly answered. "They are arriving in just a few days, Simone. My friends are here to prepare for their arrival."

Simone addressed Sagan again. "Are there only three of you from the United States? How are you going to manage taking care of a thousand people?"

Biyoudi responded for Sagan, showing slight annoyance at the question. "Mais Simone, voyons ... on a bien arrangé tout ça d'avance, n'est-ce pas, Mademoiselle Katie?"

"What's he saying?" RJ asked Sagan.

Sagan was about to translate, when Biyoudi informed him, "I am telling my wife, who worries far too much, that we have many people here to help Miss Katie with the conference. Isn't that right, Miss Katie?"

Katie smiled, her worries diminishing with every sip of wine.

"I happened to notice an armored convoy driving by the hotel this evening," Sagan said, re-aligning the conversation with his own concerns. "Have you heard of any trouble brewing?"

Biyoudi shook his head. "No. Not in Brazzaville. Only in Zaire."

"I thought you said everything was fine in Zaire," Sagan said, his antenna going up.

"Yes, everything is fine now. Everything is fine in Zaire, and everything is fine in Congo Republic. But we must all learn to call Zaire by its new name."

"The Democratic Republic of the Congo," RJ filled in. Turning to Katie now, he added, "I'm still kinda partial to Zaire. It means, *The river that swallows all rivers*."

"Please don't worry, Mr. Sagan," Biyoudi continued. "Tomorrow you will spend the morning relaxing. In the afternoon, I shall arrange to take you for a trip up the river. Then the next day we shall go to the Parliamentary Palace. We shall talk with President Lissouba. We shall make preparations for the conference. Have some more wine, Mr. Sagan. Enjoy yourself."

"Yes, Sagan," RJ said, pouring more wine into Sagan's glass, "have some more wine." Taking a sip of his own wine, RJ asked Biyoudi the only question that really mattered, at least to RJ himself. "Mr. Biyoudi, I was just wondering – is it true that the Government of the Congo is planning to be the first country to ratify the world constitution?"

"We're a little ahead of ourselves, aren't we?" Sagan interrupted. "Correct me if I'm wrong, but don't we need to have a constitution in place before we can ratify it?"

Ignoring Sagan's logic, Biyoudi gave RJ the answer he wanted to hear.

"Yes," he said proudly. "The Congo will be the first to ratify."

"That's pretty wild."

"I'm sorry?"

"I said that's going to be pretty incredible. Historic. You know. Great. I want to be there when it happens."

"Don't we all," Sagan said, aiming for sarcasm but coming up a little short.

"Yes. It's great. Very great," Biyoudi concurred. "Eat, Mr. RJ! Please! Have some more monkey!"

"Yes," Sagan encouraged RJ, heaping another serving on RJ's plate, "have some more monkey!"

RJ looked at his plate, no longer interested, and wondering how to get out of it. "I was kind of saving myself for dessert," he finally offered.

As she sat next to RJ at the dinner table that evening, Katie observed him at the business of being himself. She noted with interest that his mind never rested, that playing with his food or folding his napkin were in reality the subtle manifestations of a turbulent intellect, and she found herself longing to share his thoughts, to be privy to his mental machinations. Prefaced by a wave of nausea when his knee grazed hers under the table, she found herself experiencing the gamut of human emotions, from confusion to jealousy, to utter desolation, to some kind of grand and frightening euphoria – as if her long dormant emotions were tingling and dancing and biting at her skin in the prelude to actually waking up. Jealousy was an unfamiliar emotion to Katie – an emotion that she had a hard time accepting in others, much the less recognizing in herself. But now there was this gnawing at the center of her being with every hint of interest that RJ showed in Danielle – every hint of interest she showed in him – a discomfort, a rise of anger, even an urge to flee. And flee she did, into the beckoning depths of Biyoudi's finest wine. After a few glasses, she was able to remind herself that RJ was, after all, a young man with all the urges and needs of a young man. And she found in herself the benevolence to wish him success in all his youthful quests. Including Danielle, if fate insisted.

But this was only the benevolence of a good red wine and, as it wore off, she found herself struggling once again with a reality she didn't care to address. A reality that caused her to question the fabric of her character, not to mention her very sanity. A reality that, despite private words of self-reproach, brought needed life to her emotions. A reality that now – despite her efforts to obscure the facts – had life and definition. She was, for reasons she was not quite in touch with, attracted to him.

Dinner finally ended, and Simone invited her guests into the large room she and Biyoudi used for entertaining, encouraging RJ to put on some music. RJ was impressed to find that Biyoudi was up with the times, though his collection of LPs admittedly leaned a little heavily in the direction of Nat King Cole and Frank Sinatra. In the end, RJ decided to pay homage to Old Blue Eyes and put on the record, immediately realizing his mistake when Simone saw it as a call to romance.

"Dansez! Dansez!" she encouraged RJ, urging him toward the waiting Danielle. RJ was at first only vaguely willing but, in the end, not disinclined.

Katie, who was standing on the other side of the room having an after-dinner drink and making small talk with Biyoudi, found her concentration faltering as she watched RJ take Danielle in his arms. To add to the distraction, Sagan – who never went anywhere without his camera – was in her face, taking impromptu photographs of her and Biyoudi.

"I first met your father in 1989," Biyoudi told her. "It was in Tanzania. In the summer, I believe."

But Katie wasn't listening, and Sagan, now busy placing the cap on his camera lens, put it to her again. "He met your father in Tanzania, Katie. In 1989. It was summertime."

"Oh. Yes," Katie came back. "I believe he told me about it."

"Encore du Cointreau?" Biyoudi offered, holding up the bottle and finding it empty.

While Biyoudi hurried off to the bar to get some more, Sagan took the opportunity to turn to Katie and offer, "We could dance."

"No we couldn't."

"Why not?"

"I haven't danced since I was sixteen, that's why."

"Come on. It's a slow one. You can put your feet on mine."

But Katie declined, her heart not in it. "Thanks for asking," she said, meaning it.

Sagan took in the rejection, then said, "I was thinking the other day."

Katie waited for more, knowing more would be coming.

"I was wondering just what it is that you see in this virgin youth."

A little embarrassed at her own transparency, Katie quickly turned defensive. "You have such a way with words. Virgin youth. Not a very nice way, either." She paused only briefly before adding, "What makes you think he's a virgin?"

"I was speaking figuratively. Anyway, it was just a point of curiosity. As an incurable romantic, you know I never question love."

"Who said anything about love?"

"Ah!" Sagan responded.

"*Ah!* I hate it when you say *Ah!*" But she knew she couldn't hide from the one who knew her best, not successfully anyway, and so she confessed just enough to placate him, "I have no idea why I like him, Sagan. As if it's any of your business."

"Some enchanted evening, is that it? His laughter across a crowded room?"

"Don't start, okay? I'm really not in the mood. I feel at ease with him, if you must know. He's young and real and uncomplicated. But I'm not in love with him. I've never been in love with –"

She stopped short of finishing the sentence, not sure where she wanted to go from there, not sure if she even meant it.

"With anyone. Yes, I know. You've told me."

RJ had hung in there for the dance and now he and Danielle were moving toward Katie and Sagan in an attempt to eat up what there was left of the dance floor. Sagan decided to break in on them, just as Biyoudi returned to Katie's side, holding a Cointreau in each hand.

"Vous permettez?'' Sagan said, taking Danielle from RJ's arms and leaving Katie and RJ to stare self-consciously at each other.

After a moment, RJ said, somewhat out of obligation but also because some part of him wanted to, "Well, how about it?" and, after some hesitation, Katie took his hand. They began to dance, an awkward distance between them.

In the meantime, Biyoudi found Simone and offered her his spare Cointreau, which she took, looking on at RJ and Katie with visible disappointment.

Bridging the gap between them, RJ held Katie closer.

After some moments had passed, Katie volunteered, "It was a boy."

RJ didn't immediately get it, but she quickly elucidated.

"My baby. His name was Jacob."

Katie closed her eyes now and rested securely against RJ's shoulder, not terribly concerned that he was a virgin or a youth or some ageless and timeless counterpart to her own soul, but simply content in the warmth of his arms.

He was crazy about Sky, he thought to himself as he lay on his bed later that evening, staring up at the mosquito netting through the darkness. (He knew he needed to let the netting down, but he recoiled at the thought of being trapped by it.)

But as he lay there trying to conjure up the image of his girlfriend in his brain, she continued to elude him. He found this troubling, but strangely fascinating, given the fact that he'd always had control over her presence in his mind, and he spent a few moments trying to explain it to himself. But there was no ready explanation, and in the end – out of respect for her, if nothing else – he gathered all the pieces lingering in his memory and painfully recreated the whole picture – a jigsawed image of her he could put back in the archives for safekeeping. Somewhere in the process, he got distracted by some kind of insect flying too low over his air space – a non-mosquito variety, which was good, but unidentifiable in the darkness, which was bad – and opted for the safety of his mosquito net, despite a growing claustrophobia.

He hadn't been attracted to Danielle, he thought to himself, (there was room for Danielle now that Sky had been safely stashed away), although he had thought her pretty, and although her skin had been damp and hot to the touch and he had been stirred by it, though only slightly. But even now, the wholeness of her face, like Sky's, had somehow vanished, leaving only vague remembrances of the nuances – the smaller, unconnected pieces.

He made it a habit never to look for sleep until his mind was ready for it, until all the unresolved issues of the day had been aired out to dry. But tonight he wasn't sure what the issues were. He decided to force the sleep issue instead, covering his head with a pillow and trying to let his mind slip into the darkness but, in an unusual turn of events, his mind was reluctant to go the distance. This might be the perfect time to take a sleeping pill, he told himself. But he'd never taken one in his life, and it would follow, he didn't have any.

Best to let it all out, he finally told himself. Just let it out and get it over with. And so he turned onto his back and propped his head up and opened his eyes and let his mind have its way, its unrestricted freedom to roam the corridors of his stubborn subconscious – and waited. And it wasn't long before she appeared before him in all her pieces, and as a perfect whole.

And she lifted her head from his shoulder and looked into his eyes, and he saw that it was Katie. And he wondered about the sadness within her and about the truth of her relationship with Samuel. And he wondered what it meant that she was on his mind and keeping him from sleeping, and that he could almost feel her presence through the wall that stood so solidly between them.

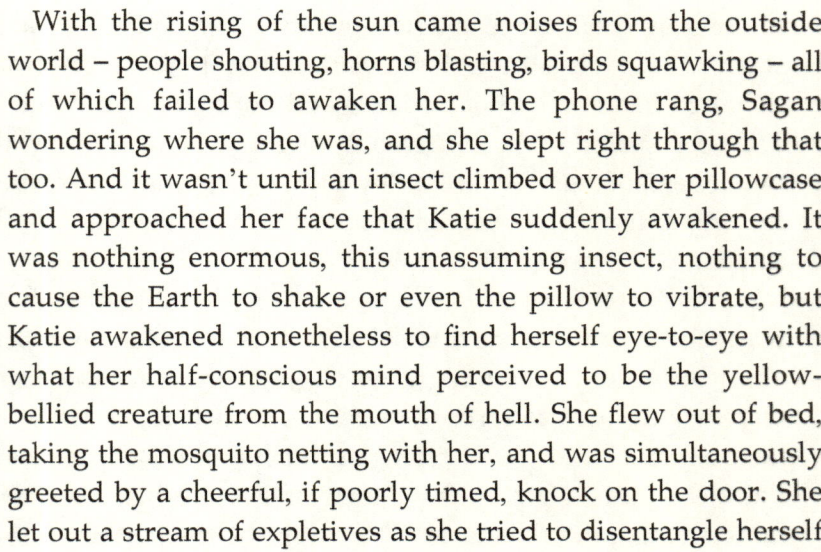

With the rising of the sun came noises from the outside world – people shouting, horns blasting, birds squawking – all of which failed to awaken her. The phone rang, Sagan wondering where she was, and she slept right through that too. And it wasn't until an insect climbed over her pillowcase and approached her face that Katie suddenly awakened. It was nothing enormous, this unassuming insect, nothing to cause the Earth to shake or even the pillow to vibrate, but Katie awakened nonetheless to find herself eye-to-eye with what her half-conscious mind perceived to be the yellow-bellied creature from the mouth of hell. She flew out of bed, taking the mosquito netting with her, and was simultaneously greeted by a cheerful, if poorly timed, knock on the door. She let out a stream of expletives as she tried to disentangle herself from the mosquito netting on her way to the door. "Crap-shit-damn-son-of-a –"

She opened the door just enough to see RJ standing there, looking one with the world in his whiter than white t-shirt and baseball cap. "Coming down?" he said, making a point not to look in the direction of Katie's mostly unbuttoned pajama top.

"What time is it?" she asked.

"Almost one o'clock."

"In the afternoon? You're kidding!"

"Yeah, I am. But not by much. It's eleven thirty. The delegates from Nigeria are here. The chairwoman. I think they're kind of expecting you to come down."

Katie shut the door, then opened it again in afterthought and called after RJ, already well on his way down the hall. "I'll be down in fifteen!"

Illuminated by the light of day, the feelings of the night before seemed pale and irrelevant as Katie prepared herself to face the ones who waited for her. She was practically two decades older than RJ, she reminded herself, focusing on all things platonic, and smiling at her temporary lapse in judgment. Had she really been attracted to him? If she had, she now absolved herself of all guilt – allowed herself blanket forgiveness. Despite an initially restless night that had culminated in a long comatose slumber, things were so much clearer today. She was much too old for him. And besides, there was nothing between them beyond the possible spark of friendship.

When she finally got downstairs, half an hour later, she found RJ and Sagan having coffee with the two delegates from Nigeria, a husband and wife, as she remembered. As she neared the table, she noted that the wife seemed to be about five or six months pregnant.

Sagan put down his coffee cup and made room for Katie at the table. "I'm sorry to keep you waiting," Katie apologized to the Nigerian couple. "I hate to admit it, but I just woke up."

"No, please. You're allowed," said the woman whose words and mannerisms exuded an almost palpable graciousness.

"We just arrived a little while ago," her husband said with a smile. "Mr. Sagan and Mr. Cutter have been entertaining us."

Katie introduced herself, offering her hand to both the woman and her husband, and thinking how kind they seemed, and how content with each other.

"Miriama Sullay," the woman said, introducing herself in turn, "and my husband, Alpha."

Katie was trying to be as gracious as she could without the benefit of her morning cup of joe, and she discreetly scanned the table for an unused cup.

"I don't think I'd trust the coffee, if I were you," RJ said, reading her mind. "Want me to get you some breakfast?"

In an instant, the sound of RJ's voice threatened to decimate her newfound judgment, and Katie found herself struggling to hold on to the rational perspective she'd so easily adopted just half an hour ago. But the pitch of his voice, deeper than his age, had set in motion a series of reverberations in the pit of her empty stomach and she could feel her emotional landscape shifting and buckling under the onslaught. *Oh, great!* she told herself, as the inner struggle turned to low voltage annoyance, and once again, the desire to flee.

"I'll get it myself, thanks," she said, taking a quick sip from Sagan's cup.

The breakfast buffet was lavish enough, and Katie filled her plate before coming back to the table, where she downed a full cup of coffee before starting to nibble on her eggs and toast. She could feel the heat of RJ's eyes on her side plate of fresh pineapple and could sense that he was having difficulty repressing his mental commentary.

"You've chaired one of these sessions before, I understand," Katie said to Miriama, choosing to ignore RJ's attempts at telepathy.

"Oh, yes. In Portugal in 1990. It was on a smaller scale, of course, but I'm sure I can do it again."

"I'm sure you can. I've heard good things."

"Will you be using interpreters?" Miriama asked.

But the heat of RJ's stare was starting to get to Katie, and she was forced to put Miriama on hold while she took up the issue with RJ, whispering to him in a fairly audible aside, "Is there something the matter?"

"I'm just hoping you're not planning on eating that pineapple," he said with great earnestness. "Because you really shouldn't eat fresh fruit here. It's just not a wise idea."

Ignoring him, Katie turned back to Miriama. "From what Mr. Biyoudi tells me, the government is planning to provide several interpreters. But we do have a couple on stand-by, just in case. Worse comes to worst, we could always use Sagan here – right, Sagan?"

"Unfortunately not," Sagan said, wiping the end of breakfast from the edges of his mouth, bound and determined not to get caught up in anything beyond his specific duties as a journalist and self-proclaimed body guard.

Katie pushed her pineapple aside and gave RJ a forgiving smile, which wasn't lost on him. She was warming to him, despite herself. Her inner struggle wasn't his fault, after all. It was she who was conflicted, she whose life was still sorting itself out. Why blame him for all the confusion?

"And what is the agenda for today?" Alpha asked.

"To relax, wasn't it?" RJ offered, flashing on visions of catching up on his reading by the pool.

"Maybe we could all share a cab and go into town," Katie suggested. "What do you think? Is there time before we're scheduled to hook up with Mr. Biyoudi for that ride up the river?" Then, aiming at the Sullays, she added, "You are coming with us, aren't you?"

Miriama instinctively put a hand to her belly and said, "I don't think so. But a short trip into town to see the market would be very nice."

"We're practically in the heart of the city," inserted RJ. "Why don't we walk?"

But in the end, majority had ruled and they had taken a cab. RJ examined the automobile as they piled in and noted with some amazement that the entire vehicle was gutted, wires exposed under what remained of the dashboard, the side panels mostly missing, the seats void of suspension, the upholstery stained and lacerated. The four passengers in the back found themselves in something of a heap where the center of gravity was the middle man.

Katie attempted to roll down a window and found the arm coming loose in her hand, then attempted, with little success, to put it back in place.

Sagan, seated up front, took charge now, asking the driver, who was reving the engine as if afraid it was going to up and die at any moment, "Combien pour aller au Marché du Plateau?" *How much to go to the market?*

After some minor haggling, they arrived at a financial agreement, and the cab took off like lightning. In no time, the driver was honking at anyone who stood in his perceived way, his horn exuding a loud, protracted sound, unlike anything RJ had ever heard before. After a while of this, RJ said it for everybody. "Well, at least the horn works."

They got out of the cab in front of the street market and managed to climb out of the vehicle, looking and feeling the worse for the ride.

Rifling half-heartedly through his pockets and coming up empty, Sagan turned to RJ for help. "Got any money on you?"

RJ handed him what he had, a couple of coins and a bag of honey-roasted peanuts from the airplane.

"Here," Katie said, slapping a couple of bills into the palm of Sagan's hand.

Pocketing the peanuts for himself, Sagan handed over the rest of it to the driver, who checked out his payment, shrugged his shoulders, then sped away.

"Am I mistaken," RJ commented, "or was that Mario Andretti at the wheel?"

"We should all stick close together," Sagan instructed the group, ignoring RJ's commentary.

"That's not going to be easy," Katie countered.

"Mr. Sagan is right. We should be very careful," Alpha concurred, taking his wife by the arm.

But Miriama put them all at ease. "We'll be fine," she said, patting her husband's hand. "Come on. Let's have some fun."

Taking hold of Katie's arm, she began to walk toward the closest vendors, who urged them forward with promises of unparalleled bargains. "Venez voir, M'ssieurs-dames, venez voir! Bon Marché! Achetez! Achetez!"

It wasn't long before the five had lost their trepidation in the excitement of the visual smorgasbord that lay before them – jewelry, clothing, baskets, carvings, and food to overwhelm the senses – eel and smoked fish, crocodile and monkey, roasted bananas, hard-boiled eggs and, of course, bottled soft drinks.

It was a photographer's feast, and Sagan took full advantage, to the pleasure of some and the disapproval of others.

In the meantime, RJ had managed to secure for himself the only thing that mattered at this precise moment, and that was, an orange soda. "Want a sip?" he asked Katie, as he caught up to her.

Katie took a welcome gulp, then commented, "I'm sweating like a dog."

"Dogs don't sweat," RJ informed her.

"You could get annoying, you know that?" Katie nudged him to let him know she was kidding, then took another long sip before handing him back the empty bottle.

As Sagan found opportunities for photographs, and Katie haggled with vendors with the Sullays, RJ kept himself busy memorizing moments, an exercise which abruptly ended when he was accosted by a badly crippled beggar who grabbed him, holding onto RJ's pants leg and looking into his eyes as if for salvation. Discomfited, RJ reached into his pockets, looking for more coins, knowing full well he had given what he had – *and more!* – to Sagan. The beggar took RJ's hand, flattening the fingers to unveil the contents. Finding nothing at the end of the line, the beggar quickly left the scene. Unnerved and acting on instinct, RJ wiped his hand on his pants leg, then checked out his leg for signs of smudge, simultaneously observing himself in the third person and hating the pristine white-man mentality that was still a significant part of his psyche, despite all efforts to undo it.

Miriama, nearby, tried to lend perspective. "I'm sure it is especially hard for you to fathom the poverty in which many of these people must live. But a true humanitarian must be willing to look into the eyes of suffering," she told him, taking him by the arm as they walked, and pressing him against her as if he were a beloved son. "You are here for a noble and worthy purpose, Mr. Cutter. To find a way to restore freedom, opportunity, and dignity to all people of the world. But don't ever forget that suffering has a face. And, likewise, so must its resolution."

RJ was touched, moved by Miriama's compassion, but frankly, confused by her easy rhetoric, and unable to respond.

"Have you bought anything interesting?" he asked after a long silence.

- 8 -

The River

 *SAGAN HAD OBSERVED THE* ups and downs of the chemistry between Katie and the bright-eyed RJ with the calm reserve of a man of experience. He felt no hurt or anger or confusion or disquietude or dejection, or any of the standard emotions normally used to describe a certain romantic suffering. He was simply and purely philosophical. Philosophical and, at the long end of the spectrum, faintly melancholy. If he had learned anything in all his travels and relationships and trials and tribulations and perceived life-endings, it was that winter never failed to turn to spring. If he believed in anything, Sagan believed in tomorrow. That being the case, he never went to bed at night without fluffing up and nestling under the blanket of hope that comes from knowing there's always a chance. In the context of that philosophy, coupled with his largely unselfish love for Katie, he found room to wish her moments and hours and even days and months of happiness without him. But the one thing he couldn't wish for – for her, or for himself – was eternity without him. Somewhere along the line, in this life or in the next, there had to be a place for him. A day, a tomorrow, when she would recognize him for what he was – the one who loved her most. A beautiful, sun-drenched Colorado kind of day when the feeling would be mutual.

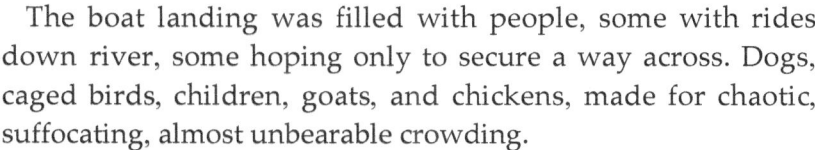

The boat landing was filled with people, some with rides down river, some hoping only to secure a way across. Dogs, caged birds, children, goats, and chickens, made for chaotic, suffocating, almost unbearable crowding.

Katie and RJ had managed to board the private boat that Biyoudi had secured for this day – not terribly modern by western standards, but sturdier than the rafts and dug-out piroques that surrounded them, and with more depth and security than the river-crossing ferries currently docked and out of service. Next to them, barges, carrying onions, rice, peppers, salt, sugar, ballpoint pens, and ginger root, were readying to take off down river, people boarding in noisy and dangerous excess.

Sagan, about to take photographs from shore, was quickly accosted by an old Congolese man who blocked the camera's view with his hand while shouting warnings at Sagan in rapid-fire Lingala.

Biyoudi intervened and talked with the man in Lingala to find out what the problem was.

"He says it's illegal to photograph the river," Biyoudi translated. "It's the state border, you understand. A strategic target."

Is there anything that isn't a strategic target? Sagan was thinking, but he said instead, "Right. I understand. How much does he want?"

Biyoudi translated the question for the old man, and they haggled briefly before Biyoudi finally came back with, "Twenty thousand Congolese francs."

"Tell him I'll give him five," said Sagan, pulling money from his back pocket reserve and not finding as much as he needed. "Tell him I'll give him four," he amended.

The old man ran off, indicating he'd be right back.

"Where's he going?" Sagan asked Biyoudi. But even before Biyoudi had a chance to answer, the man was on his way back, waving a piece of yellowed paper. He held out his hand for money now, and Sagan gave him the four thousand. In return, he gave Sagan the piece of paper and a largely toothless smile.

Sagan looked at the paper, front and back, and found it essentially meaningless and undecipherable.

"Your permit," Biyoudi explained.

"Of course."

For Katie, those first minutes on deck, the boat moving slowly down the river – not unlike RJ's carefully memorized moments – would indelibly be recorded in her memory. She would remember the monkeys playing amid the waxy leaves of the mangrove trees, the reeds swaying in the misty breeze, the congregation singing a Lingala spiritual on shore, as if to bid them safe journey. It would be an experience almost too overwhelming to her senses and, in the end, she would have to close her eyes to render it bearable.

The first words she heard upon opening her eyes again were RJ's. "Water hyacinth," he said. Two words that would forever remind her of the Congo. But now, finding RJ seated next to her, Katie offered only the blankness of her expression in response.

"Congo nu Sinnka," he elaborated. "New thing in the Congo. That's what they call the water hyacinth here."

Katie looked down at the profusion of violet hyacinth lacing the water and thought for a moment that she'd never seen anything quite as lovely.

"Someone brought it into the country in the mid-fifties, and now it's practically taken over," he told her, thinking with some discomfort how much he sounded like an encyclopedia.

"I've always been kind of partial to weeds," Katie said in their defense. "They're so undemanding."

"Yeah, they're so undemanding while they quietly take over your whole life."

Katie looked into RJ's eyes, secretly empathizing with his position on personal freedom – that was, wasn't it, what he was trying to say?

They looked out at the river now, where timber tugs had hitched a ride from a large barge in the distance, and closer to shore, a fisherman spun his net from a piroque. Katie closed her eyes again, internalizing.

RJ watched her, the breeze blowing through the wildness of her hair, fanning her open shirt. He wondered what she was thinking. In fact, he deeply longed to know, and finally came out and asked her.

"I'm not thinking," she informed him, not opening her eyes. "I'm feeling."

RJ could relate to this, and her answer gave him pleasure.

She opened her eyes now and looked at him with an intensity to rival his own. RJ studied her, not entirely sure what to make of her. Finally, he turned away, the question not resolved, and instead took his secret measurements on Sagan.

There was something about Sagan he admired, something he would want to emulate, if only he could figure out exactly what it was. But there was also, he noted, an edge to the man – a hardness – a cynicism – as if, somewhere along the line, the days of his youth had run smack dab into the brick wall of middle age and just stayed there, flattened and spent and disillusioned.

True, RJ had no concept of what it was to be fifty or eighty or in the throes of death, desperately holding on to the fleeting moments of your life. But he knew what it was to be twenty-three and to have your whole life ahead of you. He cherished his youth, fully knowing it was part of a continuum and, perhaps because of this singular insight, he had little patience for cynicism or wasted energy, or moments thrown to the wind.

He looked at Sagan again, and saw him from another angle, wondering if maybe he was wrong about him. If, in fact, Sagan carried his youth around with him the way RJ carried around his old age, not as a separate state of being, but as part of the whole. He wondered if Sagan cherished life as much as he did. Or saw it in the same way. Letting himself go the distance, he fell into wondering about Sagan's life, whether he'd ever been in love or had ever seriously betrayed his own convictions. But what he really wondered was whether, in the end – or somewhere in the middle – he would turn out to be just like him – cynical around the edges, but still surviving by the vestiges of his youthful dreams – by the faith he once had in humanity.

Moments like these were the best, he told himself as he put all thoughts of Sagan out of his mind and allowed himself to feel on his skin only the mist blowing off the river. No past. No present. No future. A sense of being one with the wind, a sense of synergy with his surroundings. A sense that time and chronological age had no bearing on reality. Absolute freedom. It ran up and down his spine like the preface to a deep and wonderful sleep, and he surrendered to it, viscerally, emotionally, and completely.

Sagan, sitting on deck, studying his environment as the prologue to a series of photographs he would be shooting in due course, pulled a cigarette butt from his shirt pocket and, cupping his hand around the flame of a matchstick, managed to light it. He looked at RJ and, for a brief moment, was envious of his youthful audacity – more than that, of his apparent insouciance. But the moment was fleeting, for Sagan had never envied youth – not even when he was living in the heart of its restless and forgiving bosom. All he had ever wanted was the independence that came with maturity – never again to be controlled by another human being or be dictated to according to someone's illusions of rank and file. And yet he couldn't deny that there was a certain beauty in the young man's countenance – a vulnerability that sprang from the very soil of inexperience and youthful arrogance – that Sagan found immensely appealing. Camera-worthy, in fact. And, snuffing out what was left of his cigarette, he took the cap from his lens and began to quietly – surreptitiously – take shots of RJ napping on deck, his long blonde hair and innocent face, in Sagan's estimation, the perfect contrast to the dark enigma that was the Congo.

"Katie!" Sagan cried out.

Recognizing the urgency in his voice, Katie ran to where Sagan and Biyoudi were standing, looking down at the water, just in time to see a massive cobra swim by, only feet away from the side of the boat.

"Yo, baby!" exclaimed RJ, now right behind Katie. "Twelve feet long, by my guess."

The cobra, long and languid, was by far the most impressive creature Katie had ever seen, and yet she felt in its presence no hint of malevolence. But as the snake disappeared into the darkness of the distant waters, Katie became aware of another presence – this one more imposing than the first one – a distant roar, an unrelenting thunder.

"Can you hear it?" Biyoudi asked.

"The rapids!" exclaimed the all-knowing RJ.

But the rapids were more exciting, more heart-pounding than even RJ had thought they would be – wild, thrashing, foaming, crashing – raging against the boulders that stood in their path. In its awkward attempt to circumvent the seething waters, the boat moved closer, until the roar was deafening. RJ found himself breathless with anticipation. *Was it some sort of death wish*, he wondered, *to be drawn to the storm, to long to be rocked in the violent arms of all that turbulence?*

But they passed around the worst of it (or the best of it, as the perspective may have been), and reached calmer waters, where driftwood and debris now littered the panorama of brown and white water.

Katie was the first to speak after a long, exhilarated silence. "That was incredible." It was a statement, and not an exclamation.

"Awesome," RJ concurred.

"Did you get pictures?" Katie finally thought to ask Sagan. But, of course, he had and they all exchanged smiles of satisfaction, bonded by the experience of having just witnessed one of nature's more majestic deliriums.

The afternoon gave way to night falling on the river. Biyoudi, Katie, RJ and Sagan sat on deck admiring the blood red sunset, as the boat navigated through the calm, dark waters, where islands sporadically dotted the river's horizon.

Sagan pointed out a hippo, mid-water, still visible in the semi-darkness, its jaws wide open in what seemed to be an endless, gaping yawn. Katie, wearing a sweater now to ward off the night chill, put down her can of fruit cocktail to focus on the hippo. She could live on the river, she told herself. She could watch hippos all night.

Meantime, RJ was getting the scoop from Biyoudi. "I was wondering, Mr. Biyoudi," he started out, "don't people ever drown in those rapids?"

"Oh, yes," Biyoudi answered. "Quite often."

"Quite often?"

"And not always in the rapids. Some of the boats that go up the river carry many hundreds of passengers. The conditions are frequently crowded, very unsafe. Inevitably, a few people... fall off.

"*Off?*"

Biyoudi did a tumble and dive with the back of his hand in confirmation.

RJ tightened his grip on the side of the boat and looked down at the murky water, dark and strangely mesmerizing under the glow of the setting sun. Eventually, he rejoined Sagan and Katie, who sat in the silence of the night air, punctuated only by Sagan's almost inaudible whistling. RJ took a seat on the straw mat directly in front of Katie, crossing his legs and displacing an enormous cockroach who quickly scurried off in five simultaneous directions.

"The snake had charmed me," he announced, looking directly at Katie.

"What?" said Katie, not getting it.

"It's a passage from *Heart of Darkness*," Sagan explained on RJ's behalf. "You've read it, haven't you, Katie?"

"Has the snake really charmed you?" Katie asked, feeling as drawn to RJ at this very moment as he felt drawn to the snake.

RJ smiled obscurely and smacked a mosquito that had come to land on his hand. "Did I tell you that the mosquitoes that carry malaria are active during the night?"

Biyoudi arrived on the scene from down below, carrying bottles of beer, which he offered to all, and which they all gratefully accepted.

RJ took a couple of pills from his shirt pocket and downed them with his beer, not unaware of Sagan's questioning eyes. "Malaria pills," he informed him, deciding not to keep him guessing. He smiled at nothing, downed some more beer, and looked out at the river, at the sunset, his blonde hair flowing in the breeze of the slowly moving boat. A youth at peace with his dreams.

Katie put her bottle to her lips, shutting her eyes in appreciation of the bubbling velvet now breaking waves through her open mouth. She couldn't remember when a beer had tasted so good to her.

She wasn't sure how long it was between that first touch of flavorful bitterness against her lips and when she first saw the *THING*. She had stretched out the beer, titillating her spirit, not just with the beer, but with all that came in contact with her senses. But at some point or another, just as her senses were merging into one giant pool of sensation built on life itself – she opened her eyes to capture the moment and saw it.

"What's that?" she asked.

Sagan got up to look and announced, "Driftwood."

Sure enough, there was an abundance of driftwood and debris floating downstream. But this was not what she had meant, and she pointed more emphatically now, and tried to clarify.

"No, I don't mean that. I mean *THAT!*"

Biyoudi and RJ got in the act, trying to figure out what Katie was seeing that no one else seemed to see, until finally Katie herself lost sight of it, and locating the *THING* became less urgent.

"What do you think you saw?" RJ asked her, his curiosity on high alert.

"Nothing, I guess. Some sort of animal. Crocodiles, maybe."

And just as she was about to sit back down, and with her the rest of them, the *THING* that Katie felt she had seen floated into view, illuminated by the sudden glow of the moon surfacing from behind the clouds. And they saw that it was, in fact, a bloated corpse, barely clothed, floating face down in the water.

Before anyone had a chance to react to the first one, downstream came the others, a dozen or more, in a slow motion parade of death – one corpse eerily the same as the other as they floated past, rhythmically bobbing up and down in the wake of the boat – a mute and macabre scenario, skillfully contrasted against one of the most beautiful sunsets the planet had to offer.

My God, Katie heard her mind say, her lips unable to penetrate the silence, her psyche calling for a stop to the grizzly nightmare.

Sagan wanted to take her hand but was not in reach of it, wanted to turn her face away from the reality of it but knew she would never have it. And so he had simply stood there, taking it in, and by rote and (he liked to think) on behalf of the human record, checked the flash on his camera and taken a series of photographs.

"Jesus!" RJ finally exclaimed on behalf of all of them. And turning to Biyoudi the way a child turns to its mother for the answers to the Universe, queried, "What is this?"

What this was, was nothing that Biyoudi had not seen before, though the sight of death had never been quite so overwhelming and quite so – well, so painfully lyrical. He answered RJ with an almost sinister flatness. "It's the war in Zaire."

"I thought the war was over," RJ said.

"Yes, the war is over," Biyoudi said, as if pronouncing the end of the world itself.

Having now seen the face of death and clearly identified it, RJ had little trouble revisiting it. After all, the hard part was the first encounter – putting your hand to the doorknob of the funeral parlor, forcing yourself to view the body now void of its soul. The body you tremble to see. And then you see it, and you know that flesh is only flesh, and you know that what you really feared was not the flesh, but the extinction of life, the death of the soul itself. Complete annihilation. And you realize in that first glance that the soul is not dead, but soaring high and free. And you realize that what's left is only carnage. *Only carnage.*

And then RJ felt a surge of nausea and had to sit down.

The trip back was entirely silent and, in its silence, entirely memorable, for they had all had the personal space and time to evaluate life and the place they occupied within it. And Sagan had concluded that, in the larger scheme of things, human life might not be any more significant than the life of the cockroach under his foot. And Katie had studied her surroundings, at times plunging into despair and at times lifted to ecstatic heights by the tragic beauty of the Congo, and had done her best to hold on to the belief that to be human was to be, in part, divine. But, in the end, she had gotten off the boat in the darkness, legs trembling beneath her, believing in nothing but the absurd willingness of humankind to inflict pain upon itself.

Was the skin a protective barrier against germs, bacteria, viruses, and parasites? Or did the skin absorb them into the system, much the way that parasitic worms could be contracted by walking barefoot? She'd heard both sides to the issue and, as she lay soaking in the small bathtub now slowly filling with water, she wondered where the truth lay. She wondered, but she didn't really care. She only knew she needed to immerse her body, to be lulled by the warmth of the water into indifference, if not into total oblivion. And if the insidious, microscopic life that lived in the water chose to enter her life through her skin – to infest and infect her – it was in the hands of a God she failed to understand.

But if God was demonic, or if he didn't exist at all, there was still good news. She had thought to bring her essential oils – oil of lavender, to be exact. Feeding it, drop by drop, into the running water, she breathed deeply of its fragrance and felt the soothing rush of sacred perfume up her nostrils. Closing her eyes, she relaxed into the tub, longing for the languid sleep of forgetfulness.

But in the end it wasn't sleep at all – to be exact, only nothingness. So she opened her eyes and looked down at her body – at her legs – good legs, she'd always felt – at her flat stomach, at her small but shapely breasts. It was a decent body, she thought, feeling strangely detached from it. It would serve her into old age, if she made it that far. But the idea of growing old on an inhospitable planet gave her no pleasure. And the view of her body as anything remotely beautiful filled her with an unnamed guilt.

The tears rolled down her cheeks, merging with the bathwater and, as she splashed water over her face, there was no telling where the bathwater ended and where her personal grief began. And she wondered how she could ever allow herself to feel pleasure again, or to love the workings of her body, as long as there were those who lived and died in darkness.

It had less to do with keeping out the insects, and more to do with a need to patch the defects, to close the gaps, to establish some sort of overall impermeability. And so, after falling into unconsciousness in the bathtub and waking up to the shock of cold water, she put on her pajamas, found that sewing kit she'd thrown in her suitcase at the last minute, sat cross-legged on the bed, and began the earnest task of sewing up her mosquito netting. And with every careful stitch of the netting, her mind began to process events and her heart began to heal. Once again she asked herself why she had come to the Congo, but the answer was no different now than it had been in the beginning. She had come to the Congo because there was no other venue by which to pay tribute to Muriel's dream. Because she knew that, for better or worse, it was a destiny she could not escape.

The knock at the door came at a point in the process in which Katie was feeling, if not healed, at least oblivious to everything but the task at hand. The knock was jolting and unexpected, and she was at first frightened and reluctant to give up the safety of her sewing. She waited to hear if the knock would come again.

It came quickly. She went to the door, holding the needle in hand as if it were, if not a weapon, at least the last vestige of her sanity.

"Who is it?" she asked, wondering what time it was. She looked down at her watch, but even squinting didn't do the trick. She wondered what she had done with her glasses.

"It's me – RJ," she heard through the closed door. And she wondered for a moment if it was really him, or simply someone pretending to be him. But then she asked herself why anyone would pretend to be RJ, and she wondered if she had grown, in the course of a single evening, certifiably paranoid.

Katie opened the door and found RJ standing there, beer in hand.

"It's two in the morning," she said, guessing.

"Two-fifteen," he said. "You really oughta be sleeping."

"Well, yeah. I was in bed."

RJ glanced at the sewing needle in her hand, but said nothing.

At some level, Katie was glad to see him, though, if asked, she would not have called it gladness, but something slightly less euphoric. Comforted, maybe. Reassured. She stepped away from the door to let him in, then returned to what she was doing. Sitting on the bed, she searched for her glasses in the bed covers and mosquito netting.

RJ entered and closed the door, then took a seat in a nearby chair. He took a moment to finish his beer before saying, "If you're looking for your glasses, they're hanging around your neck." Which, of course, they were, and Katie found them and put them on, exuding gratitude as best she could.

"I'm really not good company tonight," she told him, wishing he would go and simultaneously wishing he would not.

"Me either," he said, not moving.

Going back to her sewing, Katie noted that her hands were shaking. This hadn't happened since RJ first laid his hands on hers and the miracle was performed, and she felt some disappointment that the cure wasn't permanent. That it wasn't a cure at all. She wondered if this meant that a miracle would periodically be required, and she found herself resenting that needy part of herself that required assistance of any kind.

"Got some major holes in your mosquito netting?" he asked her now.

"Major enough."

"Umm."

RJ threw the beer bottle in the wastebasket, where it made a terrible clatter. "Sorry," he said, not exactly sorry. He watched her a while before venturing, "Are you okay?"

Katie nodded, not looking up at him.

"Cause, you know," he went on, "your hands are shaking."

Katie put down her sewing now, slightly exasperated but, more than that, feeling awkward and vulnerable. "I need to get some sleep."

When he didn't move, she insisted. "I told you. I'm not good company tonight. This morning. Whatever it is."

"I wasn't looking for company, good, bad, or otherwise. I just wanted to make sure you were all right."

"Well, I'm not all right," she said, taking off her glasses and realizing how tired her eyes were. "But I'm afraid there's nothing you can do about it."

"It's like Biyoudi said. You can't have a few thousand people killed in Zaire just a few weeks ago and not expect a few bodies to come floating down the river."

RJ's repertoire of semi-comforting words had just about run out and, besides, it was clear they weren't working. Clever words failing, he stared blankly at Katie, realizing in this moment how much he liked the slant of her eyes.

"I wish you'd go," she said.

But RJ didn't budge, just sat there, distressed and uncomfortable. He wasn't good at this. Never had been. But, despite his uneasiness, he wasn't about to leave. He wasn't sure what it was, exactly, that bound him to stay – chivalry, perhaps. Or maybe just plain stubbornness. In any event, he was determined to remain at Katie's side.

"What!" she finally cried out, questioning his right to continue staring at her.

"I don't want to leave you like this."

"Like what?" she asked. Katie looked into his eyes, trying to stare him down, but not succeeding. This he was good at. Bright with truth, his eyes looked her straight on. And she knew he wouldn't be the one to back down.

Katie's lips began to quiver now and, not far behind, the tears began to spill liberally down her face. The hole in her heart was back again, deeply aching on behalf of her own emptiness. "Why am I here?" she asked him, disconcerted to hear herself ask the question out loud.

Later in the night, RJ would awaken and, looking at her face in sleep, wonder what had taken him so long to cross the bridge between them and take her in his arms. His eyes in hers, he had felt a stirring within himself and knew then that he wanted her – though not so much wanted her as wanted to be everything to her. Wanted to be her rock and her peace of mind. Wanted to make the world a better place for her. Wanted to make the night warmer and less lonely. And yet, with all that he wanted to do for her and be for her, he couldn't bring himself to move.

Why am I here? Katie had asked, her eyes begging an answer. And it was her voice that had finally moved him, though, at first it was only his hand that had cooperated, and just slightly in her direction – just enough to invite her own hand to move in the direction of his. Which was just enough to compel the rest of him onto the bed next to her, where she held tightly to his hands and fingers, exploring them with her own. He slipped from her grip only to wipe the tears from her eyes, under which spell she seemed to pass gently into some sort of reverie, and at which point he finally put all thoughts of reason aside and took her in his arms.

"Why are you here, RJ?" she had finally asked, her fingers tracing the lines of his cheek bones, his nose, his lips, as if defining the contours of his soul.

"Here as in here-in-this-room or here as in here-in-the-Congo?" he had said, thinking only of the softness of her touch and how much he yearned for her – though, even now, he wasn't sure exactly in what way.

"Either. Both," she had replied.

Later in life, his first wife would accuse him of using political double-talk as a kind of verbal foreplay – which he readily admitted he was capable of, given the right circumstances. And so, on this night, fueled by his own uncertainty, he resorted to the refuge of irrelevance, letting the words spill freely from his lips. "Well, I'm here in the Congo because I like to think we're making history," he found himself saying. "Or I don't know. Maybe I'm here because I care about my fellow planet-dwellers and I think world government might be our only salvation. You know. There are just too many issues beyond the scope of national interests ..."

An unsatisfactory answer, judging from the look in her eyes. He stopped and tried again. "And I don't know. I'm sure it goes deeper than that, but –"

He knew it now. He could feel it hot and cold inside him. He wanted to kiss her.

And yet he had been unable to kiss her, only been able to hold her against him, aching to climb beneath her nightshirt and into the softness of her skin. She had clung to him before relaxing in his arms in an embrace so sweet that he forgot his need to kiss her. And it wasn't until she had found his lips with her own that he remembered.

They had kissed gently, awkwardly at first, then deeply and lovingly. She had left the refuge of his mouth to look into his face, his eyes, and had smiled at him through her tears – a smile which, throughout the long years to come, would never be far from his heart.

They had kissed again, this time with such urgency that he had crushed her glasses against his chest, and then had rolled solidly onto her sewing needle, which had pierced his buttocks and caused him to yell out, scaring the hell out of the both of them.

On another occasion they might have both laughed, but tonight there was little room for laughter. He philosophized instead, "Pain and pleasure... what can I say?" as he removed the offending needle from its place in the seat of his pants. And they smiled at each other briefly before wrapping their arms around each other again.

They had not made love exactly, though the mechanics were much the same – simply released all their emotions, then surrendered to the overpowering urge for sleep. She had been both a woman and a child in his arms, and as he stroked her head and let her drift into blissful unconsciousness, he wondered if it was possible that he loved her.

Mosquito netting entangling them like fish in a catch, they lay in Katie's bed, bathed in the heat of the Congo sun that poured through the window. A sudden charge of instinct awakened Katie with a start and she flew out of bed, taking the mosquito netting with her. It was becoming a ritual, this rude morning awakening. She looked at her watch, couldn't focus on it, looked for her glasses, couldn't find them, finally found them bent and tortured, put them on, and looked at her watch again. She groaned, kicked off the mosquito netting and ran to the bathroom, where she splashed water over her face, looked at herself in the mirror, and noted with interest a glimmer of child in her eyes that wasn't there the day before. And it was then that she realized that she hadn't seen or felt or in any way been in touch with that child in about as long as she could remember.

When she came back out of the bathroom, vaguely awake now and drying off her face with yesterday's towel, she stopped to take stock of RJ still asleep in the bed. And envisioning him in middle age – honed and tempered by experience – she found herself needing to turn away from the sight of him, his presence too poignant for her early morning senses.

He awakened now, stretched, looked around, frowned, found Katie on the other side of the room, figured out where he was.

"I look like hell," she told him, feeling both genuinely self-conscious and unequivocally beautiful. "You do too, by the way," she added, loving the look of him.

RJ grinned approvingly, making himself comfortable on the bed and continuing to study her.

"I can't believe I did it again," she said.

"Did what again?"

"Overslept."

"You were tired."

An understatement.

He put out his hand for her and she was tempted by everything within her to reach for it, to climb back in bed with him and, building on the night before, keep stretching in the direction of that state of bliss she longed for and that now seemed within her reach. But she couldn't allow herself the luxury. Nor could she continue to endanger her carefully guarded stability – what there was of it – even if it did depend on distance and semi-oblivion for its survival.

"Something wrong?" he asked.

"No. Nothing." She quickly dressed in his presence, strangely unselfconscious now, and he watched her, observing, processing.

"I've got to get downstairs," she told him.

"Yeah," he said, still hoping she'd change her mind.

She opened the door and looked back at him as he started to rise from the bed. But she left before he could make his way to the outskirts of her heart.

9

Civil War

JUNE 5, 1997

THERE WAS COMMOTION in the lobby as Katie got off the elevator and, somewhere in the middle of it all, she saw Sagan, who caught sight of her and waved her over. Conducting a last-minute check on the layout of her clothes, her hair, her outer expression, her very soul, she made her way through the small crowd at the reception desk and to his side.

"What's happening?" she asked. "Why's everyone checking out?" Seeing Alpha and Miriama nearby, she nodded good morning but, too pre-occupied to linger on amenities, didn't spare a hello.

"That's exactly what we're trying to figure out," snapped Sagan.

"Why? What's going on?"

"Civil war." He said it matter-of-factly, the straightest distance between two points.

Overhearing, Miriama did her best to temper his bluntness. "Let's not exaggerate the situation," she said, placing a comforting hand on Katie's arm and squeezing it gently for emphasis.

"Who's exaggerating? It's the start of another goddamn civil war." Sagan was angry now because, after all, he knew it, he predicted it, he even wondered if he had wished it just to prove himself right. And he wondered if, in wishing it, he had helped to hasten its onset. And, in having wished it and hastened it, his anger doubled as it extended to himself.

RJ arrived on the scene, looking remarkably fresh and in-the-moment. Quickly picking up on the essence of things, he reached for Katie's hand but just missed it as she left to follow Sagan into the bar area, where he heatedly heaved himself onto a couch and Katie took a seat across from him. Not easily discouraged, RJ followed and took a seat next to her, where he joined her in staring at Sagan until Sagan finally felt inclined to speak.

When he did, it wasn't to them, but to the waiter. "Primus," he ordered. "Pour trois." And then he turned to Katie and asked, "You drinking?"

"It's kind of early," she replied.

"What's up?" RJ asked.

But Sagan ignored the question to speak what was on his mind, which he directed to Katie, the object of his greatest concern. "I want you to call Norwalk. Tell him to call the whole thing off."

For the briefest moment RJ wondered – *how's Norwalk supposed to call off the civil war?* – but then he realized that Sagan was talking about the constitutional convention, not the war, and he felt the floor fall out from under his feet. For some reason, in the few moments he'd had to put his mind to work on the subject, he hadn't concluded that civil war might threaten their – or, specifically, his own – objectives. In fact, he now realized that the threat of civil war had, for him, only added to the overall excitement of the present moment. He wasn't necessarily proud of it, but there it was, and he couldn't help but look at it and be dismayed at his apparent penchant for the sensational.

"How can we call the whole thing off?" Katie asked Sagan. "We're expecting a thousand people."

"If things escalate, no one will be landing in Brazzaville. Take my word for it."

"How about filling us in?" RJ finally asked, managing to put aside his private, and largely inappropriate, concerns.

Miriama and Alpha arrived now to complete the circle of discussion, and Sagan signaled the waiter to bring two more beers.

"From what I understand," Alpha said, taking a seat next to Sagan, "it's nothing to be alarmed about. Sassou Nguesso ..."

"The dictator," RJ told Katie, opening the political side of his brain and delving into the archives. "Ruled the Congo for ten years."

"... until he was forced to introduce political reforms," Miriama continued. "Then he lost to Lissouba in the Congo's first democratic elections."

"And, of course, Sassou Nguesso claimed election fraud," Alpha finished. "It's an old story, I'm afraid."

Miriama added, "There was terrible fighting."

"Are you listening, Katie?" Sagan asked her, noting that she seemed vaguely disconnected. "Thousands of people were killed," he emphasized, finding her eyes with his own and doing his best to imprint his concern upon her psyche.

"Okay, I get it," Katie was quick to come back. "So what's going on now?"

Miriama took the question, hoping to soften the facts with the balm of her gentle voice. "This morning we heard that Lissouba sent government troops to Sassou Nguesso's home to disarm his Cobra militia. Lissouba was apparently worried about possible trouble in the upcoming elections."

Katie took this in. "All right. So Lissouba disarmed Sassou Nguesso. So maybe that's the end of it."

"No, Katie," Sagan said, doing his best not to condescend. "It's the beginning."

"I'm not sure I agree with you, Mr. Sagan," Alpha countered.

"I'm not here to argue with you, Mr. Alpha," Sagan argued nonetheless, "but –"

Katie interrupted to correct him. "It's Mr. Sullay ..."

"What? Yes. Mr. Sullay. But –" And finding his mind veering in another direction, he said out of context, " – where the hell is my beer?" He motioned the waiter again, this time with unrepressed frustration. "I've been around a long time, Katie," he said. And she hated this – the *I'm the authority, therefore you need to listen to me* approach. "And I'm telling you, this is just the beginning. We need to call this thing off and get out of here, and we need to do it now."

Still, there was something in his voice, an urgency, a brave self-righteousness, that rang danger in her heart.

The beers arrived and Sagan drank the whole of his at once. He then got up and instructed Katie, "Get ahold of Norwalk. "Tell him to get word to all the delegates. Whatever it takes. Tell him to call it off. Tell him we're coming home as soon as we can get a flight out."

Sagan left, and Katie stared after him, the fear in her stomach inching its way to her throat. She took a sip of beer to flush it down, then looked at RJ, who was busy examining the foam on his own beer, in a world alone with his deepest thoughts. She decided to leave him there.

Katie knew Sagan well enough to know that, much like a suffering animal, he was looking for a corner of the world in which to nurse his wounds. But the part of her that trusted him above all others was frightened now and, moreover, completely unsettled. She longed to go after him.

But, in the end, she decided to defer to his wishes and make contact with Norwalk. It wasn't easy to find a phone that wasn't busy, but she finally did and, to her surprise, connected almost immediately with the hospital and, shortly thereafter, with Norwalk himself.

After talking to Norwalk, Katie looked for Sagan and found him standing at a window in an empty meeting room, smoking a cigarette. She frowned internally at the sight of the smoke drifting from his nostrils, envisioning his death at the most cellular level, before the insignificance of tobacco, weighed against the backdrop of impending civil war, set in.

She came up behind him and put a hand on his shoulder, more to link to his strength than to convey any of hers. "It's a beautiful day," she said, looking out the window with him and thinking how bright the sun was and how oblivious to the troubles of the world.

"In Colorado maybe," he said, not turning around. "Did you get hold of Norwalk?"

"I talked to him."

"And?" He turned around to ask the question.

"I wish you wouldn't smoke," she found herself saying. Not waiting for his rebuttal, she followed this with, "And he says to hold tight for the moment. He says we have no way of knowing the scope of it. He says we've invested years of effort in this moment. Not to mention thousands of dollars. He says we have an obligation to see it through."

"He says, he says, he says. But he's not here is he? No, as a matter of fact, he's nice and warm and safe in his comfortable little bed."

"He's in the hospital," she reminded him.

"Exactly," he said, instantly deflated.

"He'd be here if he could. You know that."

What Sagan knew was that he was fighting a losing battle.

"Let's see what tomorrow brings," Katie said, running her hand along Sagan's arm in an attempt to reassure him, knowing full well that she was the one who really needed it. In fact, she was feeling completely unsettled, remorseful even. Why had she come to the Congo? She asked herself the question again.

Sagan shook his head and put out his cigarette under foot, never mind the carpeting.

"You can leave if you want to," she told him. "You don't need to stay for me. I'll understand." She said the words as if she meant them, but she wasn't quite sure she did. She depended on him too much to survive chaos without him. "I think it's going to be all right," she went on, not meaning it, but coating the lie with a warm smile. "I really do. We'll talk to Biyoudi this afternoon. We'll see what he has to say."

Biyoudi. Sagan couldn't help but like the man, his easy smile, his unflagging optimism, perhaps too loosely rooted in reality. But he wasn't sure what to expect from him. Katie had no choice but to place her faith in Biyoudi as the self-appointed liaison to the Congolese government, to rely on him for advice and direction. But in the heat of the present crisis, Sagan had difficulty relying on someone else's judgment, preferring his own instincts to the advice of those who purported to know best.

So when Biyoudi had stood in the hotel lobby and exclaimed, "Don't worry!" in response to Katie's carefully detailed concerns, Sagan's instincts were instantly alerted. Doing his best to remain an observer, which was his rightful place in the context of Katie's work, he had fought the urge to take her by the hand and lead her out of the Congo and back to safe ground, be it the United States or that little island off of Malta he'd read about. Instead, he had just stood there, quietly thinking about the cost of airline tickets, and wondering why life had to be so complicated that he couldn't just exclaim, *Oh, the hell with it!* and, calling things what they were, make his way to the way things should be.

"Don't worry?" Sagan had finally queried, finding the comment more than slightly inappropriate, given the current political climate.

But Biyoudi had pressed on in the same vein. "Everything is o-kay." He had stretched out the word *okay* to make two words of it, as if, in doing so, he was somehow doubling its significance.

"Could you elaborate on that?" Sagan had asked, tiptoeing ever so gently into sarcasm.

Katie would have given Sagan a look to get him back on track, but she herself was hungry for elaboration.

"Nguesso is just a flea. A small itch. Lissouba has everything under control."

"A small itch?" Sagan could feel his blood pressure rising.

"All will be forgotten by tomorrow."

"Well, that's great," Sagan had said, finding himself taking charge again, despite all attempts to remain on the sidelines, "but we have decisions to make today."

"You mustn't upset yourself over this," Biyoudi had told him, genuinely concerned. "It isn't good for your health. We will go to the Parliamentary Palace tomorrow. We will –"

But Sagan had had enough. "What's all this *tomorrow* bullshit?" he finally exploded, seeing Katie wince out of the corner of his eye and knowing he had finally crossed the line. "What happened to today?"

"Today is not a good day for the President," Biyoudi answered, maintaining his composure.

"Well, maybe tomorrow's not a good day for me," Sagan said, working his way into a confrontation he didn't feel empowered to avoid.

Which was when Katie decided to intervene and said to Biyoudi with enough gentleness to offset Sagan's rawness, "Can we go to the Palace first thing in the morning?"

"First thing in the morning. Yes. Of course." Biyoudi smiled and drew a deep breath that was revealing to Sagan, telling him that Biyoudi was not as calm on the inside as he seemed to be on the outside. "I will pick you up at nine o'clock." Biyoudi looked at his watch without actually noting the time. "But now I have to go," he added, obviously eager to do so. And, putting a hand on Sagan's shoulder, he said, "Don't worry, Mr. Sagan. Everything will be fine. We will have our meeting with President Lissouba."

Much to Sagan's dismay, Katie was visibly placated, Biyoudi having hit all the right notes with just the right roll of the tongue. Before leaving, he had turned to Sagan and asked, "Are you getting enough sleep, Mr. Sagan?"

Sagan had ignored the question, knowing that, if he dignified it with a response, he ran the risk of having the words gush from his mouth in a torrent of anger and having it all end in a flood of regret.

But Biyoudi had been persistent. "Enough to eat?" he had continued, solicitously. And, with some trouble, Sagan had managed to ignore him again.

"I shall see you all tomorrow," Biyoudi had finally said, diffusing the bomb with an ingratiating smile. "Relax, please. Put these things out of your mind. Try to enjoy yourselves."

And then he was gone, and Sagan had stepped outside of himself to take note of the back of Biyoudi's head, the shape of it, the perch of it on his body, and took stock of his long legs and confident stride, wanting desperately – whether born of artistic or of malicious inclination – to capture him on film, to assign him to the eternal paralysis of a photograph.

But Alpha brought Sagan back to the moment by suggesting, as if they were on some sort of vacation and looking for ways to luxuriate in boredom itself, that they all go down to the pool.

Whatever the actual status of impending war in the Congo, when Katie jumped skyward off the diving board, there was no outward threat beyond the blistering sun. Breaking the water, she felt the welcome rush of cold and wet surround her body and, in that moment, felt the fears of the morning wash away. She was long to come up and, when she surfaced, she took in a deep breath, as if to take in life itself. Nature was the greatest of all sedatives, she told herself, remembering why she had chosen to live in the mountains – among the trees, flowers, streams, rocks, birds, deer, elk – and , yes, even the bear and cougar. She smiled, remembering – conscious of a small emptiness that might, if given recognition, turn out to be homesickness.

She used her hand to shield her eyes from the sun and found RJ and Sagan seated at a poolside table, Alpha and Miriama at another table nearby. Sagan was smoking a cigarette and RJ, the only one in swimming trunks, was playing with the foam on his beer. Katie smiled and sent an all-encompassing wave in their direction, but not one of them took notice of her and she was briefly afflicted by familiar feelings of invisibility. But then, just as quickly as they had come, the feelings were gone, to be replaced by a sense of pleasant aloneness and an inexplicable desire to remain that way. Stretching out in the water, she floated face up, feeling both the heat on her face and the cold on her body, and listening to what she liked to think of as the pulsing of the planet in her ears. Closing her eyes, she let herself relax, merging with the womb and waiting for the dreams to come.

RJ scanned the pool for Katie's presence and found her resting peacefully on the water's surface, moving only enough to stay afloat. He was happier to watch her than to join her – so far and yet so near. He took a swig of his beer, thinking how many miles away California was. Then he turned his attention to Sagan, observing him as he deeply inhaled from a half-smoked cigarette that looked like it had made the rounds in a past life.

"Yeah, yeah, I know," Sagan said. "Disgusting habit."

"Not too recommended if longevity is your goal," said RJ, never failing to editorialize when the opportunity presented itself.

"Right now I'd be happy with survival."

"Take longevity. It's all-inclusive. So what do you make of Biyoudi's proclamation?" Unable to come to any hard and fast conclusions himself, RJ had been dissecting Biyoudi's words of conciliation all afternoon.

"What proclamation are you talking about?"

"You know. *Everything is o-kay!*" The words still rang false in RJ's ears.

"Nice guy, I'm sure, but that doesn't change the fact that he's deluding himself along with the rest of us."

"Yeah. I was thinking the same thing. Not that I've had much experience with this kind of situation, but my bullshit barometer was registering pretty high."

Sagan pinched out his cigarette and stuffed the butt back into his shirt pocket. "I'm not sure I'd call it bullshit. Wishful thinking, maybe."

"Yeah. Maybe." RJ found Katie with his eyes and noted that she was sitting on the edge of the pool now, looking right at him. "How about some more sunscreen?" he called to her, holding up the sunscreen in offering, the health of her skin a nagging concern.

Sagan, in the meantime, monitored the chemistry between RJ and Katie, deciding in the end that there was little point in laboring over something when you could come right out and ask the question, and so he said to RJ, "You like her, huh?"

After taking another long drink of beer, RJ confessed, "Yeah, I like her."

"She likes you too," Sagan said. "But you knew that."

He still liked hearing it though, having it verbalized in the light of day, in the presence of wind, sun, and sky.

Sagan got up, "Think I'll go see if there's any news."

"Keep us informed," RJ said, his eyes searching for Katie again, this time finding her neither on the surface of the water, nor at the edge of the pool. Nor anywhere in sight.

She'd been floating in the pool, gazing up at the sky, playing the games of childhood, convincing herself that she was lying on the under-belly of the planet, and waiting for the moment when she would fall into the abyss of the sky. She'd made herself so dizzy thinking about it, she'd decided to right herself and had sat on the edge of the pool before deciding to get out altogether. She'd wrapped a towel around herself and tried to skirt the reception desk on her way back into the hotel, not wanting to be reminded of any lingering unpleasantness, finding instead that she had to cope with circumventing a growing crowd. And by the time she'd found her way to her room, blue with sudden cold, she'd been unable to wedge her key into the lock. It was almost in a fit of tears that she'd finally managed to get in. But even in the refuge of her room, she hadn't felt safe or warm or optimistic. She'd taken off her swimsuit, leaving it in a wet heap in the middle of the room, quickly going back to pick it up at the sudden thought of beetles burrowing themselves into some secret part of it. Quickly dressing herself in her most comfortable jeans and shirt, and taking a seat on the bed, she'd contemplated both her inner and outer emptiness. Then she'd turned on the radio and listened to the static before turning it off again.

Moments later, she heard his knock at the door.

"Hey!" RJ said when she answered it.

She wasn't surprised to see him, only filled with longing, suddenly remembering that she had felt the same emptiness the night before and managed to fill it with this strange and simple love between them. She threw her arms around him as if the part of her, long missing, had just found its way back home.

He held her, wanting to protect her, yet feeling protected by her. Most of all, he felt warm, a warmth he'd only felt with her, and he longed more than anything to lie naked against her again. She took his hand and led him to the edge of the bed, acutely aware of the moistness of his hand in hers. Almost as much as his eyes, she loved his hands. *More* than his eyes, she loved his hands.

They were quick to fall into each other's arms again. His mind dabbled briefly with questions of morality, though why his nebulous moral code was pestering him, he wasn't quite sure. Anyway, he didn't believe in good or bad, only value and anti-value, a measure which usually served him, but which did nothing to elucidate the moment. He knew only that he was running on empty when he came to her door and that she had managed to fill him. And that somewhere in the last twenty-four hours, he'd grown both more self-aware and more self-confident. Not to mention more confused. Somewhere in kissing her neck, he reminded himself of her age and of what the future held for them. Pretty much nothing. But the smell of her was sweet, and anyway, there wasn't anything to tally but the moment. And the moment was good. He made a mental exercise of counting his blessings. One, her lips soft against his own; two, her eyes glassy with passion; three, the fragrant breeze through the window; four, their bodies in sweet and easy rhythm with each other. The tally ended there. Nothing else counted. And anyway, counting was becoming impossible.

Afterward, she burrowed into the crook of his neck.

"You okay?" he asked.

She nodded but had no ready comment.

"Want a cigarette?"

"I didn't know you smoked," she said, vaguely disappointed.

"I don't. Just thought I should ask. You know." He was hating the things that were coming out of his mouth, calculating that he sounded about thirteen.

"Yeah, I know," Katie said. It was so easy to be with RJ, so simple and sweet and uncomplicated. She longed for nothing more and nothing less than this world made up of just the two of them, for as long as it might last.

"Are you hungry?" she finally asked.

He didn't answer for a long while, giving the issue some serious thought, somewhat amazed to find that he wasn't even sure what the word meant at the moment. Still, he felt he should be hungry, even if he couldn't relate to it, so he finally said, "Yeah, why not? You wanna get something?"

"If I can move," she said, completely famished. She managed to sit up. "We could get something from the hotel restaurant."

"It's either that or the blueberry bar in the back pocket of my swimsuit," he said, mulling over the apparent absurdity of what he'd just said.

"Your swimsuit?" she asked.

"Yeah. Dumb move, huh?" He was thinking he was going to puke if he had to eat another one.

Katie got up and stood half-naked in front of him. She studied him a long time, now entranced by the sight of him, now fighting the urge to declare that she loved him for all the gods to hear – an urge that was somehow connected to the blissfulness in which she now found herself and, as such, completely overpowering. "I love you," she finally said, without plot or premeditation, and void of pretext or expectation. In fact, she loved him in much the same way that she loved the moon and stars, and declared it now as freely as she would their beauty on a cloudless night.

He stirred, then withdrew at this declaration, then resurfaced when he realized it was a statement of truth and not a probing question that required reciprocation or lies. And anyway, he wasn't sure what she meant by it, or whether she loved the child in him or the man, or whether the love was chaste or sexual, momentary or eternal. In any case, he wasn't even sure he didn't love her too, and he responded to her declaration by pulling her back to himself and tenderly kissing her mouth. And in kissing her, he felt sure he loved her, but was, in any event, too occupied to confess it.

They scavenged, but found nothing to eat and, in the end, weren't inclined to go out. Instead, they spent the evening talking, sharing their secrets and laughing at the slightest thing. Laughing felt good to Katie, sweeter than love, more liberating than sex, more cathartic than tears. And she reveled in it, carrying it to its logical conclusion – total, gut-aching exhaustion.

"We should probably get some sleep," she finally said, completely spent.

And she crawled under the covers, just as the sun was doing the same, not caring that there was an empty pit in her stomach where food should have been, nor that there was a slightly inappropriate nonchalance where her sense of duty used to dwell. Not even putting in for a wake-up call or trying to set the radio alarm, she closed her eyes and, wrapping herself around the object of her newfound happiness, ephemeral as she knew that happiness might be, prepared herself for the most pleasant night's sleep she might ever have.

Only for a fleeting moment did she think of Sagan – a moment in which his face came briefly to mind, reminding her of who she was and why she had come to the Congo, and why she shouldn't have come in the first place. Reminding her that it wasn't just her own life that she had been so free to put at peril, but his as well.

RJ reached up to release the mosquito netting, and it fell to surround them – a protective gauze separating them from the rest of the world.

He slept lightly and got up with the sun, making his way to his own room to get cleaned up, eager to know what news the day had brought.

JUNE 6, 1997 – FIGHTING ERUPTS IN BRAZZAVILLE

Katie put on her sunglasses as she passed the reception desk where guests were checking out in numbers. She caught sight of Sagan standing outside the hotel, looking impatient, and knew that she was partially responsible for his black mood. She was about to join him when RJ came up behind her.

"For you," he said, handing her his passport.

She took it uncertainly, looking into his eyes for an explanation and immediately being drawn into them and beyond the confines of her uncertainty.

"I'm feeling kind of scattered," he told her with a grin. "Thought maybe you could help."

Opening the door for her, he ushered her outside, where Sagan rolled his eyes at the sight of them, relieved even so to see them.

Tentatively, Katie tucked RJ's passport into the small bag she wore inside her shirt for that purpose, not quite awake enough to fathom the deeper meanings.

"Are we late?" Katie asked Sagan, trying not to sound too coy, and lightly running her fingers over his in playful greeting.

"Late? Ah!" he said, looking at his watch for emphasis, and making Katie cringe. "Good thing for you, Biyoudi's even later."

"Don't be in a bad mood," she said, making contact with the edge of his sleeve and tugging at it until he was forced to look at her.

He made a face, unable to rise to the task of anger, but still asked the question, directing his inquiry to RJ. "Where have you been?"

"What do you mean?" RJ said, though not in an attempt to play innocent. He just wasn't sure what Sagan was getting at.

"I tried to reach you last night."

"Last night? Like what time last night?"

"Like I don't know. Like last night."

But Sagan had a pretty good idea where RJ had been and, even if his instincts hadn't already told him the truth of the matter, their faces had.

Biyoudi pulled up in an old camouflage Jeep now, wearing a smile large enough to overshadow his tardiness.

"Good morning!" he threw out, pulling off his sunglasses to make full contact with the living.

They exchanged greetings as they piled into the Jeep, Katie still not ready to remove her sunglasses – afraid, especially in the presence of both Sagan and Biyoudi, that her eyes might betray a growing, and largely inappropriate, happiness. She sat in the back with RJ, her leg warm against his, Sagan taking the front next to Biyoudi.

"Tensions are mounting," Sagan said to Katie over his shoulder as they took off down the road.

And Katie pondered this as if she had just been presented with the world's most perplexing riddle. What tensions? The tensions in the car? The tensions between herself and himself? Between him and RJ? The tensions in the Congo? The tensions in the Universe? *What tensions?* She mulled this over for miles, obsessed by it. But she was forced to forego the obsession when Biyoudi veered too swiftly into a curve and over a pile of debris, sending everyone flying out of their seats and back again.

"Son of a bitch!" Sagan exclaimed.

"So sorry!" Biyoudi apologized, straightening the vehicle with some difficulty.

"I forgot my fucking camera," Sagan finished. Then, to Katie, "Didn't you notice I didn't have it with me?"

"You're going to blame me? Am I your keeper or something?"

They hit a series of potholes, almost ran over a chicken, then grazed a pickup truck coming at them from the other direction, overloaded with goats and Congolese passengers.

Sagan turned to Katie to throw out another over-the-shoulder remark. "Did you see all those people checking out of the hotel this morning? Well, let me tell you, those were the smart ones. The smart ones are going home." He turned back to face the road but, unable to leave it at that, turned around again to add, "Which is where we should be right now. Which is where you should be, Katie Cagle. At home in the mountains, picking those pretty pink and yellow wildflowers you love so much. That's what you should be doing, you know. Picking wildflowers."

"If I wanted to be picking pink and yellow wildflowers, I'd be picking pink and yellow wildflowers," Katie told him, irritated now, but simultaneously racked by a gnawing concern that fed on his own.

"Are you telling me you'd rather be here in the Congo, which by the way, is about to erupt into full blown civil war, than picking wildflowers in Colorado?"

"Just shut up," she finally told him, less out of anger than simply to calm him down.

RJ leaned forward now to make a request of the driver. "Do you think you could slow it down a tad?"

"We don't want to be late, Mr. RJ," Biyoudi told him, making eye contact through the rearview mirror. "President Lissouba is expecting us."

RJ leaned back in his seat again, straightened his pants and picked off a piece of offending lint.

"What do you mean – *full-blown civil war*?" Katie leaned forward to ask Sagan, forsaking her quest to uncover the meaning of *mounting tensions.*

"Just what I said," Sagan explained without explaining.

The Jeep was slowing down now, in fact nearing a crawl, as it made its way toward the Presidential Palace. Katie took off her sunglasses, noting with some alarm a congregation of armed guards blocking the entrance and coming to attention at the sight of the approaching vehicle.

Biyoudi came to a full stop, and Katie instinctively pressed her leg against RJ's.

"Whoa!" said RJ, happy to lend a leg, but even more eager to take in the architecture of the presidential palace.

A guard approached the Jeep and Biyoudi stuck his head out of the window to greet him.

"Bonjour mon frère," Biyoudi greeted the guard nonchalantly. They proceeded to speak back and forth in French, Katie translating for RJ in the back seat, Biyoudi showing the guard his papers and explaining why he was here and that the President's aide was expecting him.

"He says *no way*," Katie told RJ in a whisper. "No one's being allowed inside ...He says this is not a good day. Come back tomorrow. He doesn't know anything about the conference. He says... it's impossible ... come back tomorrow."

Sagan, taking all of this in, was about to lose it and Katie, stoked by his anxiety – the meter by which she often gauged her own – felt the blood slowly draining from her brain.

Getting in the middle of it now, Sagan snapped at Biyoudi, "Dis lui que l'impossible n'est pas français."

"What's he saying now?" RJ asked Katie, eager to understand every nuance of the conversation.

"He says tell him, impossible isn't French."

But Biyoudi ignored Sagan's request, thanked the guard, backed up the Jeep, and casually waved goodbye as he drove off.

"It's no use," he explained to everyone in the car. "There is too much tension. Tomorrow will be better."

"Please don't use that word again," Sagan told him.

"What word is that, Mr. Sagan?"

"The word *tension*," Katie filled in.

"The word *tomorrow*," Sagan corrected her.

"As you wish," Biyoudi responded. "But I want to assure you, there is nothing to worry about. Tomorrow will be a better day."

Katie reached up to put a restraining hand on Sagan's shoulder, and Sagan reached up to grasp it, clinging to it as if it were a lifeline. He held Katie's hand tightly before letting it go, then pulled a cigarette from his shirt pocket and lit the wrong end.

"Second hand smoke, man," RJ commented from the back seat.

Sagan threw the cigarette out the window.

Biyoudi, in the meantime, picked up speed and splashed through a water-filled pothole, threatening to send everyone flying out of the vehicle. This unnerving driving continued through barely-paved back streets, and RJ was about to register another driving complaint, when they turned a corner and came to a sudden human barricade in the road – three militia men – renegades, according to Sagan's instant calculations – each armed with an AK-47.

Biyoudi applied the brakes.

RJ heard someone say flatly and without ceremony, *Oh, shit*, and somewhere along the line realized that it was he. As the rebels surrounded the Jeep, he tossed the two words around in his brain, awed by their simplicity. He said them again, allowing the words to escape ever so slightly from his lips, emitting just the hint of a whisper. *Oh, shit.*

Katie, who had lost contact with RJ's leg, was suddenly filled with blood-coagulating cold, her veins frozen in icy fear. She went to reach for RJ's hand and wondered why she couldn't make the necessary connection. But then she realized with alarm that her hand had never moved – that, in fact, it was quite literally frozen in place along with the rest of her body. She watched helplessly as the rebels pulled Biyoudi from the driver's seat and threw him out of the Jeep, using the muzzles of their AK-47s to indicate to her and to the others that they'd better follow quickly, which, much to her mystification and dismay, she was unable to accomplish.

Somewhere in the midst of it all, there was a dark hole, a time and place void of consciousness. When she came to, she was standing outside of the vehicle, her hand in Sagan's, and she realized that it must have been the pull of his hand that had placed her there.

"Qu'est-ce que vous voulez, mes amis?" Sagan asked the renegades, making his best attempt at befriending them, but sensing things were not going to go well.

"Tu es français?" one of them asked. It wasn't a friendly question, simply a yes-or-no one, the answer to which might in the end decide their fate. *Are you French?*

"American," he answered, making a random choice.

And Katie, wondering why he had chosen *American* when he still carried a French passport, realized now that there was no life-saving answer—that, in fact, French or American, the outcome was probably not going to be good.

The gunman slammed the butt of his rifle into Sagan's stomach, knocking the wind out of him.

"Les americains me font chier," he told him. *Fuck Americans.* Pointing his gun at Sagan's forehead, he seemed to consider the effortless possibility of pulling the trigger. But his decision-making process was interrupted by one of his companions, who asked him in French, "What about this one? Is he American too?"

RJ listened in, not understanding the literal meaning of the words, but pretty well figuring that the finger was pointing at him. He answered swiftly and plainly, "American. Yes," then waited for the axe to fall.

The third gunman approached RJ, and RJ did his best not to wince when the gunman lifted a hand in the direction of RJ's head. But his hand landed softly and, much to RJ's distress, the gunman began to play with RJ's hair. "He's a pretty one," he sneered in French. But the other two gunmen were too busy frisking Biyoudi to pay much attention to RJ. Checking out Biyoudi's I.D. with great interest, they finally landed on the papers Biyoudi had shown the guard at the Parliamentary Palace.

Sagan, in the meantime, turned his attention to the gunman who was still in the process of manhandling RJ. "Ce n'est qu'un gosse," Sagan said on RJ's behalf. *He's just a kid*. "What do you want? You want money?"

Abruptly, the gunman dropped RJ for Sagan and began to search through his clothes for signs of any valuables. Ripping Sagan's watch from his wrist, he then proceeded to take his lighter and the few coins he had in his pocket. And while he conducted that search, another gunman began to do the same with RJ, finding only sunscreen, malaria pills, a half-eaten breakfast bar, and even less money than Sagan had had on him.

Waves of pain burned through Sagan's temples – pain that only intensified when he saw the first gunman leave a badly bruised Biyoudi to head for Katie, only a few feet away. The gunman stopped just short of her, on the edge of some emotional precipice – sanity, maybe – then thrust his hand into the front of Katie's shirt. Sagan cried out, but was drowned out by the apparent self-appointed head of the group who had suddenly decided it was time to get the hell out of there.

"Toi!" the leader said to Biyoudi, prodding him forcefully with his rifle. Biyoudi did his best to stand, though he was stunned and unable to fully cooperate. "You!" the gunman continued, forcing Biyoudi to his feet and shoving him toward the Jeep.

"What do you want with him?" Sagan spoke up, angry enough to challenge fate.

Up until now, Katie had been watching the whole affair with the kind of detachment that can only come from actual body-spirit separation. In fact, her soul had for some time been hovering safely above the scene, looking down on events from the vantage point of a kind of surreal curiosity. Only when the gunman thrust his hand into her shirt and she felt the sticky sweat of his palm on her skin and smelled the warm and nauseating stench of fish and onions and an overwhelmingly pungent tobacco on his breath, did she come back to inhabit her body and, in so doing, move to protect it. She opened her mouth to cry out and heard, not the sound of her own voice, but the sound of Sagan's crying out on her behalf.

"Ta gueulle!" the leader of the pack snarled at Sagan. *Shut the fuck up!* But then he returned to Biyoudi, pointing the gun at his head and playing with the idea of killing him outright. Biyoudi's trembling mouth tried to shape words of supplication, but managed only to mutter unintelligibly. Katie, who was on the edge of vomiting, couldn't tell if he was pleading with God or with his assailants, but the question was finally answered when Biyoudi managed to get the words out. In a voice that was both weak with pain and strong with resolve, he said simply, "I am not afraid to die." He said the words in English and there was doubt that his assailants had understood them. But the sentiment was clear enough, and Biyoudi said it again to himself, realizing with a satisfaction he'd never felt before, that he actually meant it. *I'm not afraid to die.*

After a disquieting moment, one of the gunmen began to hit Biyoudi repeatedly with the butt of his rifle, in the stomach, the groin, the head. Sagan moved to stop the onslaught but was quickly rebuffed by a blow to the face. The gunman dragged Biyoudi toward the Jeep now and forced him into the vehicle, after which the other gunmen all jumped in, turned the Jeep around, and drove off in the opposite direction from which Biyoudi had originally arrived.

Standing in the middle of the road in a state of shock, Sagan, Katie, and RJ could do little but watch the renegades drive away with their sole mode of transportation – their only real link to the Congo in tow – and stare into the muzzles of the diminishing rifles as the gunmen took aim at them, feigning to blow them away.

It occurred to RJ that it was possible that they had no ammunition and had been operating only on bluff. But what was done was done, and RJ stood helplessly with the others as the Jeep grew dim in the distance.

After a moment, Katie found the side of the road, fell to the ground, and retched unproductively.

RJ took a seat on the ground next to her. He looked at his pants legs, dirty from contact with the ground and, in an attempt to brush them off, smeared the dirt the length of his legs. "What will they do with Biyoudi?" he asked Sagan.

But Sagan wasn't quite ready to analyze events. "Come on," he told the both of them. "Get up."

Katie looked up at him, but didn't move.

"Are they holding him for ransom?" RJ persisted.

"Now." Sagan insisted. "Let's go." He lifted Katie to her feet, and RJ followed, dusting himself off as if it mattered.

Taking Katie by the arm, Sagan began to walk down the road, continuing in the original direction of their hotel. After a few moments, he began to whistle softly, a melody that seemed to transcend the continuing sound of gunfire now escalating in the distance.

It gave Katie comfort to hear his whistling and she relaxed enough to find his fingers and entwine them with her own. RJ quickly offered her his own assistance, putting his arm through hers to bolster her from the other side.

They had made their way back to the hotel in that manner – arm in arm – though how their legs had carried them, RJ wasn't sure, his own having lost all feeling at some point in the trauma. Too intent on the sound of intermittent gunfire and fearing another encounter, they hadn't spoken the whole way back. Biyoudi also pressed on their collective minds – his ordeal, his underspoken heroism, what his fate might be. Then, just as they were turning the block toward the hotel, they had heard gunfire, loud and close by, and long enough to stop them in their tracks – and, as they had stood there putting the facts together, the skies seemed to come alive with shelling. Sagan had grabbed Katie's hand, and had run with her toward the hotel, RJ losing his grip on Katie, but managing to keep up with them – to find that the hotel had been hit.

In later reflections, RJ wondered why he hadn't been able to change the course of events on behalf of Biyoudi, or why he hadn't been the one to scream out on behalf of Katie, or why, when they had run for the hotel, her hand had not been in his. Or what the gunman in question had done with his half-eaten breakfast bar, the other half of which he could have used on the road home. Or that maybe his roommate had been right when he'd said the Congo wasn't the place to go for a good time. Or how important or insignificant any of this would turn out to be in the retrospect of human history.

He thought, with remorse that seemed to grow deeper with the return of feeling to his lower limbs, that he hadn't lived up to his own expectations – or at least the standards by which he lived in his daily fantasies. But the remorse was short-lived. Why bother being sorry when there's tomorrow to make up for it? Because, in fact, at the end of the day – even a day like this one – there was still tomorrow.

Sagan, for his part, had done the ruminating, the what-ifs, the looking back upon the sins of yesterday, on their way back to the hotel, and now he was done with it. He looked around the hotel lobby, grateful to find that the damage was minor – behind the reception desk, trying to find someone, anyone, who might be of assistance. Finding no one, he turned to RJ and instructed, "Call the Alphas."

"The Alphas?" RJ asked uncertainly.

"He means the Sullays," Katie explained. "Room 322. Do you want me to go with you?"

But RJ was already off to the lobby phone. Finding it out of operation, he went straight for the stairs.

In the meantime, Sagan had located a hotel employee, apparently part of the skeleton staff still left at the hotel. "What's going on?" he asked, quickly switching to French when he got a blank stare in return.

"It's all this fighting between the government and the Cobra militia," the employee told him.

"Was anyone in the hotel injured?"

"No, but there are only a few people left in the hotel. Many checked out this morning. Others were picked up by the French Embassy just a short while ago."

"Is there a phone I can use? Can I get an outside line?"

"I'm afraid the phones are out of order."

"Of course they are." Sagan looked up at the overhead lights and ascertained that, at least, there was still electricity. "How far is the American Embassy? Is there a car we can use?"

"I don't think the streets are very safe right now. Not even in a car." But the man hadn't answered the question, and under Sagan's insistent stare, he finally said, "There are no cars."

"Can you tell me how to get there on foot? Could you draw me a map?"

"Yes, of course, but –" The boy stopped himself, deciding to be of assistance, whether it made sense to him or not, and finally taking off on his appointed mission.

"We've got to get word to Biyoudi's wife," Katie told Sagan, reminding him of her presence at his side.

"And just how do you propose we do that?"

"She'll be so worried."

"Listen, Katie," Sagan took her by the shoulder, softening slightly at the feel of her, "with any luck, they let Biyoudi go and he's made his way home just the way we did. And if they didn't – well, there's not a damn thing we can do about it."

"What about Norwalk? How am I supposed to get ahold of him to let him know what's going on?"

"He watches the news. He'll get the picture."

"But what about the delegates? What about the convention?"

"The delegates aren't coming, Katie. And if they're foolish enough to try, they won't get into the country. We're not having a convention, how many times do I have to say it? We're smack-dab in the middle of a civil war, and our only job now is to get the hell out of here in one piece." Sagan rifled in his pocket for the keys to his room and put them in her hand. "Here. Run upstairs and check on my camera for me, will you?" Katie stared at him, trying to gauge the depth of the nightmare.

"You're going to be all right," he told her. "Do you hear me? Do you believe me?"

She didn't, not really, but she obeyed his instructions, much the same way the hotel employee had, mostly because it felt good to have someone else take charge. She left just as RJ came over to report, "The Sullays are still here. They're on their way down."

And a few minutes later, they had gathered for a meeting of the minds in the hotel lobby, where there was ample room to sit, but where no one was inclined to, favoring fidgeting and pacing to sitting still. Putting their minds together, they attempted to come up with a plan of action but, in the end, were unable to come to a consensus. Yes, they needed to `get the hell out of here' as Sagan had suggested, but just how and when were still subjects of debate.

"We should wait until tomorrow," Sagan said with finality.

"Would you mind repeating that?" RJ said, unable to pass up the opportunity. "For a minute, I thought I heard you say *tomorrow.*"

"We never registered with the American Embassy," Sagan went on to close his case. "We can't call or fax out. The streets are too dangerous. We have no car. Now, maybe in the morning they'll resume the evacuation effort. Maybe – just maybe – they'll come by the hotel again to see if they've missed anyone. It seems logical to me that the only thing to do is wait and see what tomorrow brings."

Sagan took note of Katie who had her face buried in her hands, listening in without the benefit of eye contact. "Katie?" he said, eager to know that she was all right.

Katie looked up, wearing the evidence of emotional exhaustion in her eyes. "Sagan's right, don't you think, Miriama? Anyway, you don't want to be risking your life on the streets in your condition."

"Yes, Katie's right," said Alpha, immediately seeing the logic of it. "We'll stay here tonight. There are still a few employees on staff. We have food, water, shelter. It's safer for now. And tomorrow we'll see. Maybe all will be different by tomorrow."

"Yes," Miriama agreed. "Maybe it will all have been a bad dream."

The decision had now been made, and no one felt inclined to add to it. The silence that followed was chilling and, after an agonizing moment of it, Katie left the lobby, taking her apprehensions and her growing headache with her.

RJ wasn't far behind her but, by the time he had reached her room and knocked on the door, she was in the bathroom, determined to shut herself off from everyone, including RJ, for whom she might long if she were willing to let herself. But she couldn't risk the havoc his presence might cause to her shattered senses, to her wavering mental well-being and her ability to make appropriate judgments. She couldn't run to his arms now any more than she could drown herself in a bottle of wine or take a sleeping pill. No, she needed her wits about her and, even more than that, she needed time alone with her thoughts – because, in fact, she hadn't yet assimilated the events of the day.

A bath would help. With the headache and the dizziness, at least.

She heard the knock on the door and heard her name being called out and felt a faint obligation to answer. But instead, she took off her clothes and draped them over the sink, and stepped into the lukewarm bathwater.

Dinner had been a silent affair – the five of them seated around a table in the dining room – the room empty except for a handful of guests who had chosen to stay on at the hotel.

The silence among the hotel guests was shattered only by the waiter's gathering of empty plates and silverware, after which Alpha and Miriama had gotten up and excused themselves from the table without saying a word. Their exit was followed by Sagan's, then – after a long, wine-sipping interlude – by Katie's and RJ's.

Later, they'd all found their tongues and, after some discussion, had mutually decided to spend the night in two rooms – Alpha and Miriama in theirs, and the rest of them in Katie's room – a matter of safety in numbers, but also the instinctive inclination to spend life-threatening moments with those who mattered most.

Sagan had naturally taken the unused bed, and RJ had then semi-reluctantly taken residence in the other one, giving rise to the question, *where would Katie sleep?*, which she answered by lying down next to RJ. No one took their clothes off or even washed up or brushed their teeth – except for RJ who, somewhere around midnight, got the desperate urge to floss, and did so before returning to Katie's side.

Sagan felt no urge to sleep, vigilance the unavoidable price of his abiding concern for Katie. At some point in the night, he had turned to look at her – at the two of them, she and RJ, nestled together like puppies – and had been dazzled by the glow of her skin in the moonlight. Even in sleep, she wore the hint of that famous lopsided grin, and his mind was instantly transported by the sight of it to the day he first met her.

It was toward the end of the Vietnam war. Katie, barely seventeen at the time, was helping her father raise financial support for those who had chosen to leave the United States rather than fight what they felt was an especially immoral war. Sagan had come to the event more out of curiosity than to support the cause – that and because he'd been extended an invitation by Samuel Cagle, a man whose activities he had been reporting since Cagle's arrival in Paris. Not to mention that another icon of the day, philosopher Jean Paul Sartre, was rumored to be making an impromptu appearance at the underground rally on Paris's Left Bank.

She was pretty enough, Sagan noted, as he observed Katie talking to a young man – an expatriate, from the sound of his accent. But, as he studied her young face, he decided that it was the dichotomy that intrigued him. Happy and discontent, serious and unconcerned, full of darkness, full of light. He watched her, nursing his glass of wine, and eventually came to the fairly meaningless conclusion that he preferred her grin to her laughter, which struck him as false and off-key. He made up his mind he would get to know her and find out what it was about her that was joyless and what it was that was sublime. And why it was that he couldn't take his eyes off her.

After a number of aborted attempts, he'd finally managed to introduce himself and found that his normally assertive tactics met with surprising resistance. Her eyes, so warm from a distance, had quickly shut the door on what lay behind them, leaving him only to ponder the iron gate. But he'd persisted, both that evening and in the weeks to come. Jean Paul Sartre, who was smaller of stature and softer spoken than Sagan had imagined, eventually showed up but, by that time, Sagan was smitten, as evidenced by the fact that he was unable, even with the passing of time, to remember a single word that Sartre had spoken. But through the years he would remember with an almost surreal precision what Katie was wearing – from the loose-fitting red sweater that fell clumsily around her shoulders, lopsided like her grin, to the flat brown shoes in which her bare feet played. And he recalled with the singular clarity of olfactory remembrance, the sweet and fragrant smell of her. The smell that scrambled his senses when he managed to come in close to her on the pretext of reaching for another glass of wine. *Roses*, his brain had told him. He'd never cared much for roses until he'd found them blended so seamlessly with the smell of her skin.

She hadn't exactly warmed to him, but his growing relationship with her father, which he now began to aggressively pursue, guaranteed him a frequent place at their table and, eventually, she came to accept him and to look forward to his arrival. She enjoyed his conversation – this much he knew by the strength of her rebuttals, which, interestingly enough, were always played out away from the dinner table. Away from Samuel, he came to understand. In any event, it was clear to Sagan that she was attracted to his mind, to the way in which he could excite her to new levels of consciousness, and he played this card as skillfully as he knew how.

After a few months of ingratiating himself into her company and, he hoped, some corner of her heart, he began to take her out, to show her around his own special Paris, the less traditional sites and the secret corners. But he let her lead the way as well. One of her favorite sites was Père Lachaise, the cemetery where, among others, Sarah Bernhardt, Edith Piaf, and Chopin were buried. And, after their visit to this cemetery, which lasted well beyond the tolerance level of his own two feet, they began, at Katie's insistence, to explore cemeteries all over France. He was on the verge of concluding that she had an obsession with death, when it struck him that it wasn't so much death that intrigued her, but the ebb and flow of life itself. To Katie, a grave was the culmination of a story, and the story wasn't of death, but of life – life well-lived, or thrown to the wind, or spent in infamy. The re-creation of such lives through her own imagination, spurred only by the words engraved on a tombstone, was a fascinating game to her, he finally realized, because she feared, more than all else, living a meaningless existence.

After a Sunday afternoon spent reading tombstones and speculating on the lives and loves of the long-dead, they sat down at a nearby cafe for a cup of coffee (him) and tea with milk (her), where he would calculate the moments, hours, years he had yet to endure before he could finally kiss her.

The day had come well before he expected it and not on his own initiative as he had so carefully planned. Instead, she had kissed him, not because a growing chemistry between them had begged it, but because she had been suddenly and unstoppably enamored with something he had just said. It was, in fact, the irony of his life that this woman, whom he had loved from the days of her youthful prime, had, in the course of their long relationship, loved him for only one moment and only as the result of a word or two that had come from his mouth without forethought and which he could not in retrospect even recall, nor ever duplicate. Still, he had never forgotten the kiss, which was warmer and sweeter than he had even imagined, and, from that day on, he lived for the curtain call, which never came.

To his dismay, she had left the blissfulness of their world together to see the rest of Europe, and then the East, a solitary traveler in a sometimes dangerous land. He had worried about her as deeply as he could allow himself to and still retain his own sanity and perspective. Later, he'd been the one to locate her when Samuel began the sudden decline that would lead to his final days on Earth. Sagan wasn't particularly proud to admit it, but his heart had been happy to have the excuse. He'd met Katie at the airport, relieved beyond words to have her safely in his protection, hoping at some level for that encore performance, for the long-awaited kiss that would tell him what he longed so much to believe – that she might finally love him. But, instead, she had wrapped her arms around him and cried on his shoulder – not out of love for her father, but because the circle of life had been broken one too many times in her young life. And, once again, Sagan had had no choice but to rise to the challenge of remaining her understanding friend, and her comfort in time of need.

And now as she lay on the bed next to RJ, Sagan looked at her face in the glow of moonlight, and was both tortured and heightened by it. At some level, he understood and accepted her attraction to the young and unassuming RJ, who so charmingly embodied the joie-de-vivre and nonchalance so lacking in Katie's life. Nor was Sagan blind to the fact that Katie was reluctant to commit herself to anything lasting – a normal reaction to recurring loss. How could she possibly understand that, of all the people who had come and gone in her life, he himself was the true one, the one who would never leave her? How to convey this without turning her away forever?

Katie turned slightly toward him, as if drawn even in sleep by the power of his love, and let her arm fall gently to the side to hang delicately over the edge of the bed. After a moment, Sagan reached out to find the tip of one of her fingers with his own, barely grazing it in the process, careful not to disturb the sanctity of her sleep.

Then, forsaking all thoughts of a happy hereafter, he got up, put on his shoes and grabbed his camera, and quietly left the room.

TWO DAYS LATER – JUNE 8, 1997 – OPPOSING FORCES BATTLE FOR CONTROL OF BRAZZAVILLE

Gunfire and shouting in the streets could be heard from the lobby, empty except for Katie and RJ who were hunkered down on a couch, playing cards, and Sagan who stood at a safe angle to the window, smoking a cigarette.

They played gin rummy with a deck of cards RJ had gotten on the airplane, one of the gifts he was going to give to Sky on his return. One did what one could when one had no money, and he figured she would have to understand. But now it made more sense to put them to good use than to save them for the day of freedom, so he'd suggested a game of cards to distract themselves from the fear that gnawed and pressed at everyone. Besides, he had his doubts that Sky would appreciate the cheap paisley cards unless they came as part of some greater package which, so far, he'd been hard pressed to put together.

"How'd he ever end up in Topeka, anyway?" he asked Katie in reference to Sagan, intent on making small talk to counteract the sounds from the outside world.

"He won a house in a contest," she answered, happy to go there.

"Get real."

"No, I mean it. Just driving through Kansas on his merry way to Colorado. Filled out the application at a truck stop. Just for the hell of it. Six months later he's moving to Topeka. First house he's ever owned."

"So, what kind of contest?"

"Twenty-five words or less – why Kansas is heaven to me."

"No shit."

"No shit."

RJ put down his cards and got up, suddenly restless. "Gin. Let's go have some lunch." Katie looked down at RJ's cards – a far cry from gin, but okay.

"I don't think I'm hungry."

"You're hungry. You just don't know it. Come on."

RJ put out his hand to her and she took it, reminding herself how tactile the human race was, how much in need of touch and warmth.

Sagan wasn't long in joining them in the dining room, where Miriama and Alpha were already seated, and where the die-hard waiter of the previous nights, looking disheveled but still apparently willing to be of assistance, was serving them.

Skimpy ham sandwiches made up the totality of the menu, along with bottled water, which RJ was thankful to see. Lifting the top of his sandwich to take a peek at the innards, he blurted out, "Well, I guess beggars can't be choosers," realizing he sounded about as politically correct in the context of the moment as he did in college with his declarations of one-worldism. He cut the sandwich in half, then put a section to his mouth, noting with some dismay that no one else at the table was eating.

Alpha finally broke the silence. "The fighting is getting worse, I fear."

"There are bodies everywhere," said Sagan.

"What do you mean?'' Katie asked, coming to attention. "Were you able to get some news?"

"Nobody can get to them to bury them." These were the facts, and Sagan stated them with practiced journalistic detachment.

"Where did you go? When?" Katie asked him.

"It doesn't matter," Sagan said, beginning to regret that he'd said anything at all. He'd told himself, when he'd gone out in the night to investigate, that he'd keep the exploit a secret for fear of frightening Katie, but now here he was putting it all on the table. "I didn't go far." And it was true. He hadn't. The fighting had been too close and, having ventured out a short distance, he'd only managed to take a few pictures and get back to the hotel by the hair of his teeth. "Anyway, listen to me. If we're not picked up by the end of the day – if things don't improve – and I think it's safe to say they're going to get worse before they get better – I'll go to the embassy myself. Tonight. I'll bring a car back. Get some help."

"I'll go with you," RJ offered.

And Katie added, "We'll go together."

"No," Sagan told her. "It's safer for me to go alone, and that's all there is to it. Listen to me, Katie. Please. For once."

"Why should I listen to you?" Katie said, feeling the heat of her resolve rise up her neck and toward her face. "It's my life, isn't it? I'm not staying here, do you hear me? So stop playing the omnipotent, sheltering male. I'm going with you, and that's all there is to *that*."

"I'm only trying to protect you." He said this with great feeling, simultaneously realizing he was up against the insurmountable.

"I don't want to be protected," Katie said, fully aware that she wasn't being completely sincere.

Alpha intervened. "In any event, you'll need a gun."

RJ stopped eating mid-bite at the implication of weaponry, and put down his sandwich, eager not to miss the backlash.

"I thought you were pacifists," Sagan said, directing his comment to Alpha.

"It goes without saying. But circumstances –"

"Circumstances? What – you're pacifists until you need a gun, is that it? Moral until morality no longer serves your purpose?" Sagan looked at Katie as if she were responsible for this perceived hypocrisy at the heart of the Movement, just now revealed for all to see.

"You're over-reacting," she told him. "Alpha was just trying to make the point that – well, it might be safer if we had some form of protection."

"Well, excuse me, but I thought we were here on a mission of peace. You tell me, Katie. Isn't that your ultimate mission? A world in which peace prevails?"

RJ, who was basking in the heat of the conversation, decided to join in. "That's the beauty of a world united as one," he sermonized. "There is no enemy."

Sagan turned to him now, his feelings for RJ taking a sudden nose-dive. "Stay out of this, will you?"

"Leave him alone," Katie said, seriously considering throwing her napkin across the table at Sagan but, in the end, only dropping it in place.

But Sagan continued hammering at RJ, unabated. "You're beginning to irritate me, you know that? The way you paint everything with California sunshine ..."

"Hey, man, I'm just trying to make the best of a bad situation."

Katie got up from the table now, angry and disgusted. Sagan stopped venting to meet her eyes with his own and was admittedly stopped by them, but offered no apology.

"I'm going to my room," she said, shoving her chair loudly into place and leaving the table.

In the lull that followed, RJ finished his sandwich, wiped his mouth, then turned to Sagan. "You know, if you've got a problem with me, just tell me, okay? But don't take it out on her."

Sagan was about to reply that he was doing his best to take it out on him and not Katie, when he decided to keep his mouth shut instead, discretion being the better part of peace-keeping. Besides, he didn't really dislike the kid, just wanted him to grow up overnight and, if he must be Katie's temporary fix, be up to the task of it. He knew he'd been too hard on him, but, in the end, he wasn't inspired to apologize or to recant.

As he got up to leave the table, Sagan turned to RJ and said, "It seems pretty clear to me that we're not going to get picked up by the Embassy or by any other miracle or means. So if you're done eating that sandwich, I suggest you get yourself together. We'll be leaving after dark."

10

The Way to the Embassy

SHE PACKED HER SUITCASE, not leaving out a single thing, rounding up the few mementos she could find from the bathroom – an unused shower cap, a bar of soap. She bid farewell to her room, finding it a strangely poignant experience. Never again to see the walls that had witnessed her most intimate moments! Never again to touch the curtains that had breathed with her the sweet and damp perfume of the Congo. *All is fleeting*, she told herself.

Her chest tight with emotion, she was about to pull the door shut when she saw Sagan heading down the hallway toward her. Taking stock of her, he took bountiful strides in her direction. "Have you gone totally nuts?" he scolded, reaching her in a matter of seconds and ripping her suitcase from her hand. "We're walking, not taking the shuttle bus." And with that, he threw the suitcase on the floor, flipped it open, took out a few mentionables, and stuffed them into his duffle bag.

Feeling helpless and slightly disoriented, Katie didn't resist, nor did she complain when Sagan threw the suitcase back into her room and slammed the door shut in one swift movement. "Someone will come back for the rest," he told her, taking her by the hand and leading her down the hallway.

She felt like a child, her hand in his both snug and insignificant, safe and bewildered. Dropping her hand as if aware of her discomfort, he put an arm around her neck and gave her a squeeze. "I'm sorry," he said. "I'm sorry about all this unmitigated hell."

She'd almost left without saying goodbye to Miriama – not purposely, but because she had quite plainly, nearly forgotten. Begging Sagan for the few moments she needed, she had made her way to Miriama's room, at a loss for how to shape her words into an adequate goodbye.

Alpha and Miriama had decided to take their chances in the shelter of the hotel, Miriama's advancing pregnancy precluding any illusions of running through the midnight streets of a Brazzaville in the throes of civil war. They had therefore mutually opted to stay behind, a sound decision in everyone's estimation.

Katie had walked into Miriama's room, past Alpha, who had ushered her inside, and had found Miriama lying on the bed on her side, one knee propped over a pillow in an attempt to find a comfortable position. Katie was at first taken aback by Miriama's depleted appearance, though Miriama underwent a sudden transformation at the sight of Katie. And it was then that Katie realized that Miriama's face was, and always had been, chameleonesque, and that her transfiguration was invariably triggered, not by a sudden change of mood, but by the desire to be encouraging to others.

Katie had kneeled at Miriama's bedside and searched for the words she hadn't quite found in the hallway, and which escaped her still. Words failing, she put a hand on Miriama's stomach, first to make physical contact with her, then to fathom the life within her, and finally in search of signs of fetal activity.

A tear rolled down Miriama's cheek, prompting Katie's own eyes to fill with tears. "Are you crying for your unborn child?" Katie asked her.

"For all the unborn children," Miriama answered.

"It'll be all right," Katie said, caressing Miriama's cheek. "Soon you'll be home again and you'll have your baby, and nothing else will matter."

Miriama took Katie's hand and held it. "All of this madness. All our precious efforts wasted."

Madness, Katie reiterated in her own mind. *Madness.*

And Miriama went on to speak of her own childhood, random thoughts which Katie dissected both then and later, as if trying to make sense of the deceptively casual words of the prophet she had finally come face to face with at the end of a long pilgrimage.

"I was an evil child," Miriama said.

"I have a hard time believing you were ever evil."

"Believe it," Miriama said. "I was the bane of my mother's existence."

"She told you this?"

"I was the last born, you see."

"Out of how many?"

"Fourteen."

"Well, maybe your mother was just tired of having children."

"Who could blame her?"

"Fourteen might have been an imposition."

"A curse."

"Where is she now – your mother?"

"I think it made me strong – being born a curse," Miriama said, not wanting to talk about her mother's predictable death from a lifetime of overwork and malnutrition. And then Miriama said out of context, or so it seemed to Katie, "Do you know what she used to tell me – when she would brush my hair and I would scream?"

Katie couldn't help but wonder why Miriama had chosen this particular story to frame her farewell. "She used to say, *Miriama, you must be willing to suffer if you want to be beautiful!*"

"And did you want to be beautiful?" Katie asked her, squeezing her hand and noting for the first time how delicate her fingers were.

"Yes," Miriama answered. "But not that badly."

Katie had been unsure what to say next, only known that she wasn't ready to leave her newfound friend behind. And Miriama had filled the silence with, "Alpha is a good man, don't you think?"

"Yes," Katie had quickly answered, realizing she'd never given much thought to the man, though she'd thought him pleasant enough, and presumably genuine. "I'm sure he is."

"If there is one thing I am sure of, it is the love of this man."

"That's good," Katie had said weakly in response.

Miriama had then looked deeply into Katie's eyes as if to penetrate her soul, resulting only in Katie's discomfort. If Miriama was trying to tell her something about herself, Katie didn't really want to hear it – wanting on this dark and fearful night only one thing – to connect to, and to be warmed by, Miriama's presence. Anything beyond that seemed not only superfluous, but bordered on the unpleasant.

Miriama had relented with a smile and they had talked a few moments more before she had kissed Katie's cheek and said in parting, "Be safe."

"I wish I didn't have to leave you," Katie had said, after which she had tagged onto this cri de coeur, "I wish I could get to know you better."

"Be safe," Miriama had reiterated in place of goodbye, gently running her fingers over Katie's cheek.

Safe. Katie had repeated the word in her mind, practicing it at the edge of her lips, and making a mantra of it all the way down the stairs and into the lobby where RJ and Sagan awaited her. Stepping outside of the hotel was like stepping off the face of the planet, the door opening wide to reveal the uncertain. Sagan had walked out first, carrying his camera and duffle bag, followed by RJ, carrying his own duffle bag, and Katie carrying nothing at all.

Simultaneously, Sagan and RJ had reached for Katie's hand and, in the split second that was the other side of eternity, Katie had weighed the choice against the full measure of her life – Sagan's hand, strong and enduring – RJ's hand, eager and compelling. And in the end, she had taken RJ's for no better reason than because – determined to start living up to his own expectations – RJ had taken hers before she had had a chance to calculate the whole of her tomorrows.

Sagan hadn't argued the point, simply led the way through town, now and then driven by the unnerving journalistic instinct to take photographs of the carnage – the twisted, lifeless bodies, the looted shops, the wandering animals, the frightened people darting through the shadows and into the alleyways, seeking refuge from the fighting.

In all of this, Katie thought only of RJ's hand, now loosening its hold, now holding her tightly. She wanted to drift away, leaving her body to fend for itself, but was grounded by contact with his hand to a harsh and unspeakable reality. Not allowing herself to make visual contact with the images that surrounded her, she watched him instead – awed by his apparently casual strength, which she knew now was not obliviousness – and by his gentle courage. She felt the stirrings of an almost spiritual selflessness borne of brief contact with his all-knowing eyes, and found herself praying for his survival above all others. Above her own.

Above Sagan's. He – this young and beautiful youth – this man of tomorrow. This hope of the future. Above all others, he must live.

According to Sagan's street map – which he continued to study at intervals even though he'd had the layout memorized for some time – only a dozen blocks separated them from the American Embassy and the luxury of letting down their guard or, in Katie's case, totally falling apart, which she planned to do as soon as circumstances permitted. Darkness had fallen heavily on Brazzaville and visibility was limited, making the prospect of walking twelve blocks more than a little daunting, particularly considering the imminent dangers.

The pain in Katie's stomach was new – a pinching of her intestines, a cramping that threatened to cripple her. Sagan stopped at the next corner to see how she was doing and whispered, "We're not too far now. Around the corner, a few more blocks. Straight down Avenue Foch. Stay close to me. Both of you."

She was going to suggest a short respite, during which she would breathe deeply in an attempt to alleviate the tightness in her chest and the increasingly agonizing pains in her stomach, when gunfire erupted from across the street. Katie had never heard gunfire from such close range before, and the sharpness of it was jolting.

They took temporary cover behind the nearest perceived shelter – an overturned pull-cart that did little to hide them – and, after a moment of bargaining with death, they decided to take off again.

As they surfaced, a man and woman ran out of the shadows and across the street, the woman concealing a small child in the folds of her dress. Another round of shots lit the scene, and Sagan watched helplessly as a spray of bullets felled the whole family. Vaguely aware of his own jeopardy and that, somewhere in all of this, Katie and RJ had run ahead of him, he found himself unable to make the decision to move. He watched as the child – like the phoenix rising from the ashes – got up and looked around in solitary wonder. Unable to fathom anything more than the fact that its mother would not take him in her arms, the child began to cry – the only life now remaining in the street.

Sagan stood staring at the child – all concerns for his own safety overshadowed by the immensity of the moment. His fingers started to move around the periphery of his camera as if, somewhere in their own sphere of existence, they sensed the perfect picture. But in the end, Sagan didn't take the shot. Instead, he ran into the street toward the crying child and did his best to find a place for it in his arms, holding it against him and rocking it with all the instincts of a parent.

Sensing that Sagan was not with them, Katie and RJ slowed their pace and came to a stop. Katie turned and caught sight of Sagan and, covering her mouth with her hand, stifled the impulse to scream.

"What's he doing?" RJ wondered out loud. "He's gonna get himself killed."

And Katie, who could stifle no longer, finally yelled out, "Sagan!" so loudly that her voice broke, stabbing the back of her throat and making further outbursts impossible.

Protecting the child with as much of his own body as he could, Sagan started back across the street and was thrown headfirst onto the sidewalk when mortar suddenly hit just feet away.

The deafening explosion, followed by a long round of shooting, sent Katie and RJ, in an act of pure instinct, running for their lives.

When the smoke finally cleared, Sagan looked through the haze for signs of Katie. What he found instead was her conspicuous absence. Stunned, but apparently unhurt, he now took stock of his own peril, the way ahead no longer an option. Quickly deliberating which way to turn, he took the child, ran down another street and disappeared.

Looking back for Sagan from a point of relative safety, Katie said, "Where the hell is he?" turning to put the question to RJ and noting with some horror the blood-covered side of his face that, somewhere in all the chaos, had been ripped open above the eye. "Jesus!" she exclaimed. "Oh, my God. Look at you."

RJ tried to stop the bleeding, but with little success, and the sight of blood on his own hands was making him queasy. "I'll be okay," he said in an attempt to convince himself.

Katie rummaged through RJ's duffle bag and found a bandana, which she pressed against the wound. Replacing her own hand with one of his, she urged him to apply as much pressure as possible. "Come on," she said, feeling sure that her bowels were going to explode, that she was going to crumple up and die an agonizing, embarrassing death in the middle of Brazzaville proper. But she had neither the time nor the luxury of crumpling, folding, or in any way checking out. Taking RJ's free hand, she began to lead him away from the madness, casting a brief backward glance in the faint hope of seeing Sagan appear out of nowhere.

- 11 -

The Embassy

HIS NAME WAS JOHN MORRISON. A sharp-looking diplomat with a take-charge attitude and manners that harked back to another era, he'd been stationed at the U.S. Embassy in Brazzaville for nearly two years when the latest civil war had broken out. Holed up at the Embassy, he'd spent a lot of time reminiscing about the days leading up to his assignment in the Congo Republic. About how a simple nod of the head had brought him to another side of the world where the sun scorched the sky and the rules were entirely different. He'd been thinking about that – about how different things were back home and how much he'd love to be there – when Katie Cagle walked into the Embassy, holding onto the young man with the badly lacerated face.

Tending to them gave him something else to think about – something besides his own regrets and the small, but consistent demands of other foreign nationals who were gathering at the Embassy seeking refuge from the war. Something about Katie's face reminded him of his fiancée – the one who'd written him just a week after his arrival in the Congo to tell him it was all over. The one who couldn't tell him to his face. The one he still thought about, though not with any real affection.

He had introduced himself, then escorted the young man to First Aid to get some stitches. He could have put in the stitches himself – he was, after all, a bona fide physician. But he was tired and, anyway, he was more interested in finding out who they were than in treating the boy's wounds. Consequently, he had left RJ to the care of others and taken Katie to a small side room where he suggested she and RJ hole up for the duration. It was a room he had reserved in the back of his mind for that special, but unforeseen situation – a room he had apparently reserved for today. He had pointed out the small sink in a corner of the room where Katie could clean up, and he had waited outside the door for her to finish. Then he had led her to his office, intent on finding out the details of their ordeal. Who was she? Who was the injured boy? Who were they to each other? And what were they doing in the Congo at this most inauspicious hour?

Katie sat across from John Morrison's desk, looking tired but clean. He sat a little too casually to the side of his desk, studying her as she sipped from her coffee cup – tiny sips, *sipettes*, he was thinking – not really drinking at all.

"Good coffee, isn't it?" he ventured. "Chicory, actually, but who's complaining?"

Katie nodded, taking another sip.

"I have to admit I'm still not terribly clear on what you're doing in Brazzaville," he continued. "But I suppose in the scheme of things, it really doesn't matter, does it? You're an American citizen in good standing. And all you really want is to get home in one piece. Would you say that pretty much sums it up?"

Pretty much, Katie was thinking, and she nodded her assent.

"Pretty much sums it up for all of us," John Morrison said, more to himself than to Katie. He stared at her, making her feel self-conscious, but unable to help himself. He realized now he'd played it too softly, too furtively. He realized he hadn't learned a thing about her and probably wasn't going to unless he changed his tack.

"Is there anything I can get you? Anything you need?"

Katie grew restless in her chair now, trying hard to stay awake, but beginning to give in to a bone-deep exhaustion which was the aftermath of acute stress and which mere conversation could not rival. Still she managed to answer his question. "I could use some clothes. A toothbrush, or –" All of her possessions were with Sagan, she realized. Strangely enough, the thought gave her comfort.

"I'll take care of it."

"My friend... is he?" RJ's oozing wound was on her mind right now – that and sleep and a chilling fear that her conscious mind wouldn't let her put a name to. But she forced the thought to the top of the page, adding, "I'm afraid I – I don't know what happened to –"

"Mr. Cutter? Ought to be cleaned up by now. Shall we go see?" There'd be other opportunities to satisfy his curiosity, he was thinking. The war wouldn't end tomorrow.

But it wasn't RJ she was thinking about now, but Sagan, and she finished the thought in her own mind. *I don't know what happened to Sagan.*

"Is there something the matter?" he asked her, noting the distressed look on her face. "Something else you wanted to tell me?"

She nodded, unable to move her mouth to elaborate.

Morrison waited. *Patience*, he told himself. *Patience and she'll give you the whole story.* And he wanted a story, less because it mattered in any practical sense than because he had been here too long and he needed a good story – an American tale, a tale of home and familiarity. And besides, he was hungry to know what she was really like, this woman who reminded him of love and kindness and gut-wrenching betrayal.

"We lost our friend," she finally told him.

"I'm so sorry," he said, genuinely saddened at the thought of another death remotely in proximity of his own control.

"No, you don't understand," she said, explaining herself. "He isn't dead." And she went on to relate the story, more briefly than Morrison would have liked, but displaying the range of emotion he had looked forward to and expected of her.

"Well, I'm very sorry you got separated," he said when she had finished. "It's a hell of a time to get lost. Hell of a place too. But I think there's reason to feel hopeful he'll turn up. Probably before the night is through, if my gut is on target. Which it usually is, you know." He said this, knowing that his intuition as of late had failed him more often than it had steered him right. Not to mention that his gut wasn't speaking to him tonight, at least not in ways that gave rise to hope and happy endings. "What's this about world government?" he asked, throwing it out there, titillated by the idea that Katie might be part of some subversive plot to overthrow her own government. Truth was, he'd heard of the Movement, heard of plans to host a convention in the Congo. Still, the thing was unclear to him, and the inferences on his end had been largely negative.

"What do you mean?" she asked, quickly jumping to the defensive.

"Earlier you mentioned that you were here to host some sort of world government convention."

She had earlier opted to tell him the truth, figuring that, under the circumstances, there were more pressing concerns than her political leanings, but still vaguely uncomfortable about sharing this part of the story with an Embassy official. Now she wondered if she would live to regret it. "Yes," she said, abbreviating her answer to one word, annoyed that she should have to once again feel guilty about her efforts to bring the world together.

"So what's it about?" he asked. "A plot to take over the world?" He wasn't pleased with the sound of his question and, by the look on her face, nor was she.

"I'm tired," she said.

"I understand," he responded, aware that he had probably gotten as much information as he was going to get from her in one evening. "Shall we go see about the boy?" Taking note of the perplexed look on Katie's face, he added, "The young man you brought with you. The one with the injury?" He found himself putting a hand to his eye to touch the site corresponding to RJ's wound. *It's going to make a nasty scar*, he thought to himself.

She hadn't thought of RJ as a boy, and it hit her like a revelation, shocking and slightly dismaying, that anyone else should see him that way. "RJ," she said, finally getting it.

"Yes. Mr. Cutter. Shall we see to him?"

Morrison opened the door for Katie and ushered her into the next room, where a dozen or more people – mostly Americans – sat, stood, meditated, snoozed, smoked, and nervously whiled away the time. They largely ignored Katie as she walked through the room, Morrison behind her.

Katie's eyes quickly landed on RJ, standing at the back of the room. His face had been stitched both above and below the eye, the blood washed from his face, and she was thinking he looked pretty good under the circumstances. She threw her arms around him, relieved to see him alive and essentially well. Eager for the security of his arms, she pressed herself firmly against his blood-stained shirt.

Morrison looked on, still curious about the relationship between them, but not getting very far in his mental audit. "Like I told you," he said to the two of them, "it's kind of fend for yourself around here. Let me know if – well, you can take care of yourselves, right?"

Morrison started to walk away when Katie called after him. "When do you think we'll be evacuated?"

"It's only a five-minute shuttle to Kinshasa. You'd think it'd be a simple thing but, unfortunately, it's not. Still, with any luck, we'll get out of here tomorrow."

"But –" Katie started.

"Yes?"

"I'd like to wait for our friend."

Morrison said nothing, only gave a quick smile, doing his best to convey encouragement before leaving the room.

Katie turned her attention to RJ now, to his face, patched and swollen, and she put her arms around him again, rocking him back and forth in an attempt to comfort the both of them.

After a long moment, she pulled away, wiped her tears, and looked into RJ's face. Suddenly he wasn't looking too well. "Are you all right?" she asked.

When he'd lost sight of Katie, Sagan had had this feeling his life was about to end. The smoke had cleared enough for him to see that she was gone, that she had left him, maybe forever. He'd wanted to follow her, run after her, but he knew he would never make it through the impasse of concrete and rubble that stood between him and all that mattered to him in life – that stood between him and the rock upon which he had built his fortress. The child in his arms made the task, if not impossible, at least extremely unwise, and he had no choice but to renounce the idea in favor of the child's survival.

As fate would have it, the narrow street he chose in a moment of pure instinct led him into still greater danger and he found himself caught in the crossfire of rebel insurgence. With nowhere to turn and nowhere to hide, he had done his best to shield the child who, most incredibly, was now fast asleep in his arms. *Sleep is a blessing*, he found himself thinking, glad for the child and envying it too.

And just as he had been sure that death was upon him, and he had confirmed once again the fact that, even in death, he was not a praying man, the woman he would come to know as Nzinga appeared out of nowhere to pull him from the fringes of existence and back into life again.

RJ sat on the floor of the tiny bathroom, hunched over the toilet, vomiting. Katie sat next to him, rubbing his back and watching him retch.

"You gonna be all right?" she asked taking advantage of what she hoped would be at least a brief interlude. But RJ quickly went back to vomiting and was unable to answer the question. "It's been awful," she said, feeling a need to put a label on it.

"Yeah," he said, managing between spasms to add, "No shit."

Someone knocked on the door, wanting to use the bathroom, and RJ answered by heaving into the toilet.

"We're sick in here," Katie yelled out to the interloper, finding it interesting that she had chosen to advertise RJ's illness as a joint venture.

He was there a while, retching and holding her hand, before he felt it might be safe enough to leave the safety of the toilet. Bracing himself against the wall, he got up and, leaning on Katie, allowed himself to be led back to the room they now called home.

The room was, in fact, no larger than a walk-in closet – a window, a chair, a cot, a sink. Katie closed the door and helped RJ onto the cot, noting that he was sweating profusely and beginning to shake uncontrollably. She covered him in blankets from head to toe but, in short order, he'd kicked the covers off again.

Katie wet down a rag in the small sink. Going back to RJ, she began to wash his face, doing her best to circumvent his wounds. Then she wiped down the rest of his trembling body, hoping to soothe the heat of his young skin. She was worried. About infection, mostly. About his dying without ever saying another word. *What were his last words?* she asked herself, placing some importance on remembering them. She wanted to laugh when they finally came to mind. *Yeah,* he had said, vomiting into the toilet. *No shit.* She looked into his eyes, which now seemed to her a paler blue, as if the pigment had faded along with his life force, and she wanted to kiss him for all that he had been to her. *No shit.* She repeated his final words in her brain and fought the urge to laugh out loud, knowing full well that to do so would be to open the flood gates to a full and possibly irreversible breakdown.

RJ closed his eyes in exhaustion and Katie turned now to look outside the window, where the moon was rising over Brazzaville and where mortar fire, like giant, sparkling fireflies, lit the late-night, early-morning, sky.

Katie turned around again just in time to see RJ shoot up in bed and stare straight at her. But it soon became clear that RJ wasn't looking *at* her, but *through* her. She followed his gaze across the room, finding only the bare wall at the end of the journey. Turning around again, she was surprised to find RJ on his back and apparently fast asleep. Unnerved, Katie went to the sink to rinse out the washcloth and saw by the light of rocket fire, paratroopers parachuting into Brazzaville. It was a spectacular sight – silken jelly fish floating in gentle synchrony through the dark green and lavender sky.

She was late to answer the door when Morrison knocked a few minutes later. "I hear the boy is sick," he said in a whisper that he had a hard time executing. "Sorry I couldn't come by sooner. It's been ..." He trailed off, deciding not to focus on his own problems or his own weariness.

The boy, she was thinking. *The boy*. But the word smacked more of truth at this moment than it did of insult. Lying there, sick and vulnerable and unconscious, RJ was not only a boy, but a lamb, a cherub, an innocent.

"I was going to try to find you," Katie told Morrison, more than ready to share the burden. "I think he's really sick."

"May I come in?" Morrison asked, and Katie stepped aside to make way for him. "Not much room in here, is there?" Morrison apologized as he slid past Katie and into the room.

"No. It's wonderful, really," Katie said, knowing they had been blessed with a privacy that was in short supply under the circumstances. She directed her words to Morrison, but her eyes couldn't help but stray to the window where parachutes could still be seen floating into the open mouth of an angry Congo.

"Reinforcements," he commented, noting her distraction.

"Reinforcements?"

"The French."

Morrison took the chair next to RJ's cot and put a hand to RJ's forehead, quickly retracting it.

"He's hot, isn't he?" Katie said, afraid to hear the verdict.

"He's hot," said Morrison.

Somewhere in the night, Katie had moved her chair to the window and, after much torment, fallen asleep to the sounds and sights of war-torn Brazzaville, above which the sun was starting to rise. Her dreams had been of chickens and goats and dust and debris – of standing at the precipice of the inferno...

... while his dreams were of falling in, landing in the fire and not being able to find his way out. It had been hot there, so hot that his skin had blistered and pussed and sizzled and, in the end, peeled away and left him raw and agonizing. It was hell, all right. And just as hot as his mother's favorite preacher had told him it would be. In fact, it was hotter. And just as he was surrendering to eternal damnation, out of nowhere, the rains came. A drizzle at first, followed by a raging torrent. And his raw flesh had cooled and softened, and he knew that the healing could not be far behind.

RJ stirred and opened his eyes, landing almost immediately on Katie. He wasn't sure where he was exactly, but somehow it didn't matter much. He smiled, knowing he was alive, knowing the nightmares were behind him.

Katie opened her eyes and turned to look at him. Her heart leapt at the sight of him – his eyes still pale but somehow brighter than the night before, and she returned the smile warmly, quickly going to his bedside to sit next to him.

RJ did his best to sit up. "Wow," he managed. "I feel like total crap."

Katie brushed RJ's wet hair away from his face. "You look like it too," she said, relieved beyond measure to hear his voice.

"How long have I been out?"

"Long enough to worry me. Just what I needed, you know. A little more worry." In fact, the severity of RJ's illness had sent her into a tailspin of worry. What would life hold for her if RJ were to leave this world? He who represented all that Muriel had believed in and given her life for – faith in the future of the world, faith in humanity. In no way was she ready to lay him to rest – not the true believer – not the young man she loved so dearly, nor the hope for the future he had come to represent. And certainly not on the tail-end of losing Sagan to a dark and frightening unknown.

RJ looked down at his clothes, noting that they weren't his own, noting that they were wet.

"The fever broke," she explained. "You've been sweating like a dog."

RJ remembered the original conversation, the trip to the city market, but right now he wasn't up for the repartee. "Shit," he said, all the facts beginning to gel. "Don't tell me. Son of a bitch. I've got malaria!"

"My first thought – given all the anti-malarial pills you've been taking, coupled with life's wonderful penchant for irony. But our resident physicians find it hard to believe you could have come down with malaria so quickly. They say the incubation period is twelve days to several months, so it's probably something else. The flu maybe. Or maybe some spoiled food. Or maybe you got some bad water."

"Yeah, well trust me – on the low end, the incubation period for malaria is a matter of a few days. That and the fact that new strains of malaria are resistant to drugs, and bingo – I qualify!"

His voice was weak, but Katie was heartened by his quick and excited speech – evidence the worst was over. "Well, they can't exactly run diagnostic tests from the Embassy," she told him, "but..."

His own whereabouts suddenly dawned on him and he looked around, taking it in. "But what?" he said after a moment.

"But just to be on the safe side, John's been giving you some kind of sulfa drug."

"Sulfadoxine? Fansidar? Okay. That's good. Who's John?" Suddenly exhausted, RJ fell back onto the bed.

Placated by the knowledge that RJ was going to be all right, Katie found her mind wandering toward the unthinkable, and she directed her gaze out the window.

RJ joined her from his prostrate position, and said, "Still no sign of him, huh?"

Katie shook her head, fighting the urge to give in to her worst fears.

"He'll show up," RJ said, kissing Katie's hand and trying to find reason to believe his own rhetoric. "Like I told you – the guy's immortal."

JUNE 10, 1997 – EVACUATIONS SUSPENDED DUE TO HEAVY FIGHTING

Cup in hand, Katie made her way through the ever more crowded room that had quickly become the Embassy's main waiting room. She found her way to the other end, where John Morrison had just poured himself a cup of would-be-coffee. Katie joined him to find the pot empty. Noting the situation, Morrison handed her his own just-filled cup.

"I couldn't," she said with a smile, gratefully taking it.

He took the empty cup from her hand and filled it with water for himself, then asked, still trying to get a handle on the whole affair, "How's your friend?"

"Did I ever have a chance to thank you? He's doing fine."

"Well, listen, keep the room for the time being. Til we need it for someone in worse shape." He added after taking a sip of water, "And pray we don't."

"So tell me what's happening," she said, watching his eyes for signs of duplicity.

"What's happening is, we're on temporary suspension as far as evacuations are concerned. The cease-fire's apparently fallen through and fighting has escalated around the airport. If the Red Cross can't even get the bodies out of the streets, there's no way we're going to get all these people out of the country. I wish I had better news for you." And when Katie seemed relieved, he added, "Or is that better news?"

No duplicity there, she was thinking, *and yes, it's better news.* "You didn't tell me about the paratroopers ..."

"Deployed by the French to help with the evacuation efforts."

"Where'd they come from?"

"Bangui. Libreville. Gabon."

"Any word on how it's going?"

"What – the fighting? It's hard to get a reliable account. But the feeling is we'll get out of here eventually. Tomorrow maybe, if all goes exceptionally well."

Katie sipped at her coffee, looking around at the multitude of people waiting anxiously for evacuation.

"Can you imagine what the French Embassy looks like?" Morrison said, giving her shoulder a comforting squeeze before walking away.

She watched him leave and wondered what workings of fate had brought him to this juncture. Standing in the relative safety of the American Embassy, awash with a fear she couldn't quite shake, she waited for the rest of her life to unfold. She felt completely out of control and was suddenly overcome with the urge to fall on her knees in prayer.

Instead, she decided to tend to RJ.

He was better, that much was for sure – no longer a breath away from leaving the Congo the easy way. But he was still very weak and his appetite was poor. Katie spent the day at his side, keeping the conversation light and manageable, and trying not to venture into Sagan territory, or into speculating about the hours to come. During RJ's frequent periods of sleep, she studied him – his full and pleasant mouth, the almost fragile thinness of his body. She loved him, that much she knew, and thought him beautiful in all the ways that mattered. But if she was in love with him, it wasn't with the turn of his mouth or the pallor of his skin or the blue of his eyes. If she was in love with him, it was with his youthful innocence and with the part of him that belonged to a distant future – neither of which was hers to keep.

When evening turned to night, she opened the curtain, just enough to let in the moonlight, and unveiled a serenity that was broken only by occasional bursts of rocket fire. She helped RJ sit up in bed so that she could brush his hair, a task she reveled in.

RJ cringed when Katie hit a knot in his hair, and she carefully brushed it out, reminded of Miriama's mother's words, *You must be willing to suffer if you want to be beautiful...*

Katie put down the brush now and got into the cot alongside him, curling up next to him in silence. "You know I love you," she whispered.

"Yeah," he said, finding the words slipping from his lips a lot more smoothly than he ever thought they would. "I love you too."

She looked into his eyes, devoured by his gentleness, and kissed him softly.

"Aren't you worried about getting malaria?" he asked.

"I didn't think it was contagious" she said, uncertain. "It isn't, is it?"

"Not as far as I know." He was playing with her. "So I mean, if you want to kiss me again, I guess you can."

She smiled, settling into the crook of his arm. After a moment, she looked up at him, studying him.

"What?"

"Nothing.

"Tell me."

After a moment she found the words and said, "I see your beautiful face and I say to myself, *His whole life lies ahead of him. Like a journey down the Congo River.*"

"Did something happen to us while I was sleeping?" he asked, detecting a subtle atmospheric change in their relationship.

She gave a small shrug.

"I want to know."

"I guess I just realized how much I want you to be happy."

"Well, maybe happy isn't what I want to be," he said, still not sure what she was talking about, but fairly certain he wasn't in accord with the general sense of it.

"Everyone wants to be happy. It's fundamental. What do you want to be if you don't want to be happy?"

He thought about it and came up with, "I don't know. Impassioned, I guess."

She smiled at him and he returned the smile.

"Hey, Katie?" RJ spoke after a long moment.

"Hmmm?"

"Can I ask you something?"

"Almost anything."

"I mean – don't take this the wrong way, okay? Has it always been that one-sided?" He knew *she knew* what he was talking about, so he cut to the chase. "I've always wondered – from the first time I met you two. I mean, it was always pretty obvious the guy had a thing for you. I just never could tell – you know – if the feeling was mutual."

"I don't know how I feel about him," she said, only wishing things were clearer. After a moment, she added, putting an end to the query, "Maybe we should get some sleep." She felt RJ's lips gently graze the top of her head and rested easy, knowing the case was temporarily closed.

Looking out the window from the safety of his arms, she found herself communing with the face of the moon. *One Earth*, she thought to herself, reflecting on the motto that had brought her to these unpredictable shores. *One Earth. One moon. One moment in time.*

That he was still alive was nothing short of a miracle. That he was safe and warm and cared for got him to thinking beyond the realm of miracles and into the mystic workings of destiny itself. Where had she come from – this dark and sensitive creature whose empathetic eyes were among the gentlest he'd ever known? And why had she chosen to risk her life to take him in? Had she surmised, glancing between the cracks in the shutters, what he himself was unaware of – that the child he held so close to him was not, in fact, asleep, but was back in the warmth of its mother's embrace? For, pulling Sagan from the streets and into her home, the woman had gently taken the lifeless body from his arms and laid it to rest on the floor, and Sagan had observed that its final Earthly expression had been a sweet and peaceful smile.

It was only then, when the woman looked up at Sagan – seeing in him some mysterious but damaged hero – when she came to him and, looking into his eyes, put a hand to his side to staunch the bleeding, that he realized that he was hurt. And realizing it, he decided he might as well own it, and owning it, he observed himself slipping into unconsciousness.

When he awoke, he found himself prostrate and in some pain, but neatly bandaged and in the comfort of a veritable bed. The child's body was nowhere to be seen, having been apparently disposed of during his unconsciousness, and it was only after searching his brain that he decided the child had actually existed in the first place. A hot rice soup was fed him by the woman, and an attempt at verbal communication eventually led them to a solid impasse. She spoke almost no French, nor any English, her own dialects lost on him entirely. From what he could gather, she was alone. Alone and terribly frightened. Had there been others in her life, lost in the turmoil of recent days? This he failed to discover, though he believed it to be the case, as it was obvious to him that her mental and emotional wounds were still freshly oozing.

By contrast, his own wounds, as it turned out, had essentially been superficial. Shrapnel had penetrated his side, neatly exiting his back without any serious damage beyond the threat of tetanus and infection. Still, he'd done enough bleeding to send his head reeling when he finally sat up from the bed, anxious to urinate and get going. But it was obvious from the continued sound of gunfire from the streets that he would not be leaving soon and that he might as well take advantage of the woman's kindness to regain his strength. Then, when the time was right, he would head out again, find the Embassy, meet up with Katie and RJ, get the hell out of the frying pan and, with any luck, not land in the fire.

He wondered if they'd made it. Chances were they had – the Embassy wasn't that far away. And anyway, he preferred that fantasy to the one in which they lay dead in the street to rot in anonymity among the others. He preferred the fantasy of Katie's smile – too rare in the last few years, but still vivid in his memory. Drifting in and out of consciousness that first day, he thought of her often – always – only. Of the kiss they had once shared and of how much he wished he could live the moment again or, in lieu of that apparent impossibility, be absolved forever of the agonizing curse of loving her. And yet, absolution was not really what he sought as he lay in the damp and musty-smelling bed, willing his angry wound to heal. For the curse of loving her was all he had and, in that curse, like a seed that lays dormant under the freeze of winter, he recognized the germ of his own salvation.

The voice does the Buddha's work. It was a phrase she'd read somewhere in the course of her life and now it came back to her the way thoughts do when the brain decides, for reasons that are usually quite unclear, to recycle them. And so she was thinking about the human voice, about how it projected a person's character in its purest, most essential form.

In short (as best as she could figure, it all boiled down to this), she missed Sagan and longed for the sound of his voice. She had prepared herself as best she could for the possibility of his death – for the possibility of never seeing his face again – but it had never hit her until this very moment that she might never again hear his voice – scolding her, laughing with her and at her, doing his *Ah!* thing just to annoy her – that, in dying, he took it all with him, and with him to the grave the lilt and undulation of his words, and the feelings and thoughts that they stirred within her.

It surprised her and, more than that, it frightened her, that she could imagine nothing more agonizingly painful than this – never to hear him speak her name again.

"What are you thinking?" John Morrison asked her. He'd been watching her for some time from across the crowded room, watching her stare out the window at the embassy guards and at whatever might lie beyond them, and he walked up to her now, touching her lightly on the arm to bring her back to his own sphere of existence.

"Oh," she said, turning. "Hi." A nice face, she was thinking, though she wished he wouldn't interrupt her thoughts, which were prayers more than they were ruminations. "I was just – nothing, really. Staring, I guess. It's strangely quiet out, don't you think?"

"I wish you wouldn't stand so directly in front of the window."

There he goes again, she was thinking. *Fussing over me.* But, in fact, she didn't mind the attention.

"I hope you don't mind," he said. "I'm something of a worrier."

"I gathered that," she said with a smile.

"How's your friend?" He asked because it was conversation, but also because he still hadn't sorted it out.

"He has a name, you know."

So why do I refuse to use it? he asked himself. Not coming up with an answer, he said to Katie instead, "RJ, yes. Does it stand for anything interesting?"

When she was slow to answer, he pre-empted, "Listen, don't mind me."

Suddenly feeling awkward, Morrison started to walk away, when Katie grabbed him by the arm. "I'm sorry," she apologized. "I'm being rude, and I'm not even sure why. I think it stands for Randolph Jeremiah.'' And in saying his name out loud, she felt RJ come to life, as if by speaking the whole of his name, he had finally stepped out of the periphery and into the main circle – as if he had gone from pencil to ink in the book of her life. And she realized that, come what may, he would always be a part of her and she a part of him.

"Sounds – impressive. Have you know him long?" He knew he was pushing his luck, probing beyond the parameters, but the question was still there and, God knew why, he had to ask it.

She sighed loudly, not out of exasperation, but simply because it was a thing she'd been finding herself doing in the framework of all this waiting. So he wanted to know who RJ was – or, more obviously, he wanted to know who RJ was in the context of her life. Given the world situation and the largeness of their immediate crisis, it mattered little to her that he should know. "Through this – *whole thing*," she said.

"This whole thing?" he asked, confused.

"He's a delegate. We met in Barcelona and flew to the Congo together. For the convention. I told you about it."

"So you've only known him a short time?"

She was thinking that a short time was a relative thing, but she didn't want to go into it, so she said instead, "We've gotten to know each other pretty well."

Why does that make me uncomfortable? he was thinking. But it did, and at the risk of throwing salt into the wound, he probed, "Pretty well?"

"He's a good friend."

He searched her eyes, looking for more.

"And more than that," she said with finality, meaning only that they'd been to hell and back together.

"More than that." He repeated the words as if, in doing so, their nuances would take shape and provide him with a clearer picture.

"It's a crazy thing," she said, trying to find some definition to her own feelings. "All this upheaval. Everything looks different to me now. Do you know what I mean?"

"Are you in love with him?" Morrison suddenly asked, discovering in the asking a sincere concern for her circumstances. He quickly added in an effort to mitigate his impertinence, "I ask because it's basically none of my business."

She smiled, strangely unaffected by Morrison's prying. "You know," she said with a grin, "there's only so much I'm willing to tell a total stranger."

"Are you saying you still think of me as a stranger?"

"I'm saying you haven't told me a thing about yourself."

And he realized in that moment that he hadn't. That he hadn't, in fact, shared his deeper thoughts with anyone, not verbally, nor in writing, for approximately two full years. And it was only now, in his longing to know more about this American woman who intrigued him so, that he realized how much he wished he could share of himself. That he realized how truly lonely his recent life had been.

For the first time since he'd left his apartment in California, headed for the airport and the great adventure that lay ahead, RJ was feeling genuinely homesick. Not for Sky, exactly, though once in a while he found a smile creeping across his face at the sheer absurdity of her, at her frenzied, self-aggrandizing ways that, for reasons obscure, always did something to ring his chimes. Not for her affections or even her companionship, but just for the familiarity of her presence. The way he longed for seafood pasta on the pier or for the Very Berry Blitz at the juice bar. Oh, God, to be living in the familiar! The banal! The mundane! Oh, for the life of peaceful oblivion!

He looked around him at the prison that was his room at the American Embassy and, taking stock of the cumulative effects of his life – now culminating in a stifling, unfamiliar present – he realized that it came down to just this: he'd give his left arm for a good movie – preferably science fiction – or even a good old-fashioned love story. Or a good joke, for that matter. He wanted out of the serious and into the lighthearted. He was too damn young to feel so goddamn old. Call it what you will, he wanted to get on a plane, plug in the earphones, and go home again.

Nzinga was perhaps the most beautiful woman he had ever seen. He said this to himself, knowing that his assessment was heavily colored by the fact that she had single-handedly nursed him back to health and that he was, quite naturally, in love with his protector. Still, her eyes were magnificent, her skin dark and honeyed, her smile sweet and reassuring. He would love her if he could. He would stay with her if things were different, and make sure she was safe and protected in turn. He toyed with this idea, which came and went, invariably strengthened by her proximity, her gentle tending to his needs. And he wondered why he would leave her when he could love her and – he somehow sensed it – be everything to her. When he could finally know the joys of intimacy and reciprocity.

She helped him sit up in bed, smiling at him as she handed him the bedpan of sorts, and turning away to let him do the deed. That done, she took the bedpan from him and went to empty it, coming back in short order with a small pot of water and a rag. To wash him with, she indicated via the rudimentary sign language they had managed to use with some success. And then she helped him with the washing, bracing him against the less-than-tepid water with her smile. He could love her, he told himself again, fighting the urge to take her hand and pull her down to him. He could love her, but not here, not now, not in the present. He could love her, but only in another dimension, in another world where the facts and reverberations were different. And besides, he still hadn't ascertained the truth of her life, the truth of who might be walking in the door, or shooting it down for that matter, at any moment. And what that could mean to him. Or to Katie, whose safety was his self-sworn duty, and to whom he was destined to remain eternally emotionally faithful – not because he wanted to necessarily, nor because he believed in blanket fidelity – but because things were the way they were.

She tended to the wound with a gentleness that was next to godliness, her touch on a par with the flutter of butterfly wings. The pain had diminished, he realized, chancing a look at the wound itself and finding that it was beginning to heal. The pain had diminished and the wound was healing and the world outside was strangely quiet, causing him to speculate that a cease-fire might finally be in effect. *Life is good*, he told himself, rethinking only briefly his stance on the Universe itself. And he looked at her and made a point of finding her eyes, which were – sign language notwithstanding – still their most effective means of communication. And with his eyes he told her what he had just finished telling himself. The time had come for him to go.

JUNE 12, 1997 – MASS EVACUATION OF FOREIGN NATIONALS BEGINS

It was a strange thing – to want more than anything to get the hell out of the Congo, and yet to long with your very soul to stay forever. And now, as John Morrison prepared himself to evacuate the Embassy, he found himself clinging almost desperately to the moments, both past and present, of his life in hell. And hell began to take on the shape and form of something sweeter. *The man was right*, he told himself, *who said that things that are bitter to endure are often sweet to remember*. For already the bitterness was turning sweet and he longed for the sweetness to endure and not to be parted from it. Thoughts and images raced through his head – the Congo River, boiling and mysterious, the fragrance of hyacinth in the air, the orgy of tastes and foods from which he had initially shrunk and had even disparaged, the unrelenting sounds of life that had driven him to an early distraction. Would he ever again feel so alive? But there was no choice but to take advantage of the temporary cease-fire that would finally allow civilians to evacuate. Take advantage and be grateful for the chance that might never come again.

And so, putting all regrets aside in favor of the performance of his duty, Morrison made his announcement, buoyed by the audible and communal sigh of relief in the room, and by the tentative smiles of anticipation that quickly followed. That done, he searched for Katie's face in the crowd and found only RJ.

How to tell her, RJ was thinking as he made his way to their room, knowing she would not want to leave without Sagan but would have no choice in the matter. He'd been self-centered and cowardly, he told himself as he opened the door to find her sitting by the window. Thinking only of his own escape from the ugly monotony of present circumstances, he'd completely forgotten to think of her or of Sagan.

She turned when he walked into the room, and he thought he would break into tears at the sight of her and at the message that he had to convey to her.

"We're evacuating," he said, opting for brevity.

Shortly thereafter, Morrison knocked on the door and opened it to find Katie in RJ's arms, the both of them in tears. "We're leaving in about fifteen," he said, choosing not to linger.

Katie and RJ pulled away from each other in silence. RJ returned to his packing, now half-finished. His tidiness was taking on new dimensions, Katie noted with the superior clarity and total lack of relevance that seemed to be the flip side of crucial moments. And indeed, RJ had become obsessed with precision-folding and smoothing the non-existent wrinkles. He hesitated before putting his passport into his duffle bag, then stuffed it deeply into the side pocket. Putting his bag over his shoulder, he found Katie and looked her squarely in the eye. He felt his strength returning as he told her, "I know this is going to sound flip, but here's the thing. The guy is immortal."

"No one is immortal, RJ. If he were alive, he would be here."

"And I'm telling you not to give up on him, okay? For all we know, he's on his way back to the States as we speak."

"I know him. He wouldn't have left without me."

He wanted to hug her, to comfort her again, but he sensed it was not the thing that was going to get her out of the room, and so he said instead, "Well, maybe he had no choice." He held out a hand to her and urged, "Come on. We'd better get going."

Stepping away from the window was probably the hardest thing she'd ever had to do and, in the final analysis, she found it impossible. How could she step away when there was someone coming down the street – someone big and tall and – wearing a camera? Her hands began to shake as she strained to bring the figure into view.

RJ joined her at the window, his own hope feeding on hers. But as the figure became more distinct, they saw that it wasn't Sagan after all, but a soldier, carrying a rifle. As the realization set in, they watched the soldier turn onto another street and disappear from view.

Katie's disappointment was visceral, her desperation more excruciating than ever. She fought to regain control of herself and managed with some effort to win the outward struggle. She turned to RJ now and said, referring only to the part of her that was still alive to say it, "I'm ready."

It took a surprisingly long while to load the evacuees into the convoy of jeeps, trucks, and other vehicles, already crowded to capacity with other foreign nationals, as they prepared to make the life-altering ride to the airport. RJ gave

Katie a hand as she stepped into the back of the last truck. He'd given her that much. To be the last one to go. He figured it would make a difference to her in years to come.

He wondered what she was thinking, her face drained of color and expression. He figured she wasn't thinking anything, only feeling, as she had once said, that day on the river. He wondered now if feelings weren't the thing that killed us in the end. And he pondered the irony, for he knew that the gift of feeling was the only thing that made life worth living at all.

He held her hand as the convoy began its short journey, and they sat in silence at the back of the open truck, facing the world outside – a decimated Brazzaville, devastatingly quiet under the cease-fire. Oddly enough, there was no conversation among the evacuees, as if all had chosen the world of feeling over the world of conversation. Only a whisper here and there, perhaps a prayer.

To have the moments back again. This, in the end, was what Katie was thinking. For she wasn't feeling as much as she was thinking. Somewhere in the dark of her conscious mind, she recognized the cruelty that she had inflicted upon Sagan – not because she had failed to love him, but because she had failed to appreciate his love for her. She wondered what she would do with the rest of her life which, at some level, unappreciated and unexplored, had always revolved around his great and undying affection. She wanted to stop the convoy, to shout his name – not in agony, but as a tribute and a final farewell. *Sagan! My good and eternal friend!*

Nzinga put the bicycle in his hands and he wanted to laugh at the irony of it. On another day, in more benign circumstances, he would have put his mind and hands to fixing it – adjusting the brakes and straightening the handlebars, inflating the wheels and maybe even polishing the rims. But he took it now with gratitude and, in taking it, fell in love with it, as it would take him more swiftly than his own two feet to his ultimate destination. Just as importantly, it came from her – Nzinga – which, to him, had come to mean, *the one who has saved me*. He rang the bicycle bell, surprised to find it working. She laughed and he laughed with her, a world of conversation in the moment. *Bells and horns*, he said to himself, as he stroked the bicycle seat and readied himself to leave. *When nothing else in the Congo is working, you can always count on horns and bicycle bells.*

He wanted to kiss her, not sure of the protocol. But in the end, caring little for protocol, he kissed her gently, parting from her only with the utmost difficulty. If he were a praying man, he would have prayed for her well-being, for her reward. But he was not a praying man, only a man trying to do his best to live life as he saw fit, and with nothing to offer her but the honesty of his affections. Her lips trembled as they tried to form the semblance of a smile, succeeding in the end to convey her deepest wishes, despite the haze of tears in her eyes. "I love you," he told her, knowing that the words were meaningless to her, but figuring even so that no translation was necessary. And anyway, he said it not so much for her understanding as for the Universe to hear. If there was a God or gods or some exterior or internal Law, then they – it – should stop and listen and know, and put an arm around her in his stead.

Doing his best to hold on to both his camera and his duffle bag, he got on the bicycle and, experiencing great pain, both physical and emotional, rode away from Nzinga forever.

But life being the unfathomable mystery that it is, Sagan found his pain almost instantly replaced with an overwhelming anticipation that bordered on absolute joy, for he knew beyond a doubt that Katie was still alive and that, come what may, he would find her. The belief that he would see her again was the closest thing he'd ever known to faith, and he had no way to explain it, nor did it matter to him. He only knew that, inherent in goodbye, he had found the seed of hello, and it grew within him with every inch of ground he covered. Had the air ever been this fresh, the sky this blue, the sun so bright overhead? He would have reproached himself for feeling joy in a setting that would make others sick with revulsion and disgust. But he chose to ignore the destruction, the trail of death, and even the very real danger that his visibility in the streets of Brazzaville still posed to his life. Most interestingly of all – and he pondered this with some personal satisfaction – he wasn't inclined to take pictures of what he normally would have seen as a photographer's feast. The destruction of Brazzaville. An exposé. He could see the spread and he instantly rejected it in favor of living his life.

He rode on, vaguely aware that – prompted by his insistent pedaling – the bleeding had started again. The blocks, short by normal standards, were long and arduous, and he wondered if walking might be the way to go. But he was afraid of the process, afraid it would slow him down or weaken him beyond his present weakness. And anyway, the Embassy wasn't far now. Just a couple more blocks.

Riding in the back of the truck, Katie couldn't help but take note of the sun's brightness, and she wondered if it was rational to be resentful of a celestial body. She was thinking of this, wishing at some level for the sun's own demise, when she saw the man on the bicycle. Bicycles brought Sagan to mind, and she would rather have buried him now than have him come to mind, as the pain was setting in and threatened to overwhelm her. But she found him hard to ignore, this man on a bicycle – this fast-approaching mirage. Resisting the urge to hope, she viewed the man's advance with wary detachment. And besides, she didn't trust her own eyes, nor her overworked imagination. And so she looked the other way and went back to wishing the sun would have the decency to hide behind a cloud. Except that there wasn't a single cloud in the sky.

There are moments in time that are indelible, and the instant that RJ caught sight of Sagan riding down the street toward them was one of them. No mirage to him, Sagan was real, hiding the depths of his emotions behind his normally-annoying whistle. RJ looked at Katie, waiting for the glorious moment of recognition, only to find her deliberately looking the other way.

"Look!" he said, pointing toward Sagan with zealous insistence.

And she looked only briefly before turning away again.

"Look, goddamn it!" he insisted, physically turning her head, and simultaneously wondering how to stop the convoy.

She finally looked, then came back to his eyes for confirmation, then stood, banging her head, and started to jump up and down, alarming everyone in the vehicle.

As RJ would later remember it, her face had exploded in some sort of other-worldly ecstasy, the likes of which he had never seen before. He had managed with some success to restrain her as she fought to get out of the moving vehicle. But his efforts had been in vain, and when the vehicle slowed down to turn a corner, she had clambered out. Gratefully, she'd survived the exit.

In all the commotion, someone had alerted the driver and he'd come to a stop, giving RJ the opportunity to witness the reunion – that old-fashioned movie he'd been longing to see.

Katie had run toward Sagan with all the abandon of a woman in love, and Sagan had gotten off his bicycle and gently nudged the thing aside to make room for her arrival. Reaching him, Katie had checked herself, stopping short of his arms. They had looked at each other as if for the first time in heaven, and then he had slowly taken off his camera and duffle bag and put them on the ground next to him to make room for her in his arms. She was stopped by the sight of bleeding from his side, and had been visibly alarmed by it, but Sagan had managed to allay her fears with a shrug of the shoulders, a disarming smile, and a few well-chosen words to which RJ was, unfortunately, not privy. Finding him in other ways quite intact, Katie had apparently had no trouble believing him. By this time, the truck driver was honking his horn and, not quite as moved by the love story as RJ was, the evacuees had begun to protest, wanting, understandably, to move on. RJ had tried to quiet them, these noisy spectators at the theater, then gone back to viewing the scene, just in time to see Katie throw herself into Sagan's arms and kiss him with a passion born of absolute clarity. Sagan had returned the kiss, at first with an intensity born of deprivation, then slowly and lovingly, enveloping her in his arms as if to absorb her into his own body.

When Katie and Sagan had finally pulled away from each other enough to see each other's faces, they had begun to laugh out loud to the degree that RJ wondered in earnest if they had lost their mutual minds. But then he realized that it was only a case of life handing them so much happiness at one time that the surplus had no other way out. And in that moment RJ had felt all the pangs of melancholy that come with vicarious pleasure and had made a secret wish that someday he himself would know the kind of love that he was now witnessing from the back of a well-used truck in war-torn Brazzaville. And then he had realized that the movie was over, and he had jumped from the vehicle to throw his happy arms around the both of them.

"I see you picked up a souvenir," Sagan had told him, reminding him of the wound above his eye.

"Oh, yeah – that. Right." And for the first time, RJ wondered if he would have a scar. And he thought maybe he wouldn't mind having one – that, worse than having a scar, would be having nothing tangible to remember it all by.

On the way to the airport, they had sat next to each other, molded together like sardines, she holding hands with both of them, her face all flushed with happiness. And RJ had taken the opportunity (Sagan's current focus on Katie) to study Sagan's face, still wondering what it was about him that he admired, apart from his obvious survival skills. He wondered too why his own feelings of the moment were not appropriately placed – why it was that he felt neither jealousy, nor reproach, nor a desire to de-throne his replacement or, at the least, challenge him to some sort of show-down. He wondered why, instead, he felt only gratitude, relief for Sagan's safety, and a deeper sense of love than he had ever known before – for both of them. Maybe it was because he had never been in love with Katie to begin with. But then again, he wasn't sure he hadn't been. Maybe it was simply the upheaval. The war. The upside-downness of it all. And yet he recognized the stirrings of what he would come to think of as nobility, and he noted it, and it gave him for all time a point of easy reference, so that in moments of self-recrimination, or when decisions weighed on him from all sides, he would remember what it felt like to be a truly honorable human being.

12

Maya Maya Airport

JOHN MORRISON WATCHED the evacuees being assembled into the airport to wait for their shuttle flights across the river and out of the country, overseeing, as best as he knew how, those areas for which he felt responsible. The small airport was filled with people, most of them done with processing and showing of passports, and seated where they could find the room, all but the children wearing flat expressions that spoke of exhaustion and lingering apprehension. *It will all be over soon*, he told himself, finding little personal comfort in the thought.

He'd heard the story by now – about the last evacuee who rode up to the truck on his bicycle and hopped in while the truck was still moving – coincidentally to find himself in the arms of his lover. He wasn't sure how accurate the story was, as it wore the cardinal signs of retelling and inevitable embellishment. It made a nice story though, and he had quickly discovered, upon brief investigation, that the hero was the missing American – the man that Katie had been waiting for. And he was pleased to know that life sometimes had its happy endings.

He made a point of seeking them out, finding them in the airport crowd, the hero's arm around Katie's waist, and he decided, in that first glance that frequently told the tale, that he could have liked the man had circumstances allowed him the chance to get to know him.

"So far, so good, as far as the cease-fire," he said, addressing all of them at once. "Let's hope it holds."

Warmly, Katie shook Morrison's hand. "I want you to meet Sagan," she said with unreserved enthusiasm. "My missing friend." *Friend*, she told herself again, the word taking on greater dimensions than she'd ever thought possible.

Morrison extended his hand. "John Morrison. Glad to have you with us." And it was at this point that Morrison noted the blood on Sagan's shirt. "You okay?" he said, shaking Sagan's hand, but thinking only of the blood and how it stirred in him the urge to mend and heal.

"I'll be fine," Sagan said, convincing him only slightly.

"Well – I've got things to attend to. Just wanted to be sure and say goodbye. Wish you all the luck."

"Thank you, John," Katie said. "You've been wonderful. I won't easily forget you."

"Nor I you." He said this with some emotion, which he did his best to conceal, then added, "Colorado, huh?", his parting words to her a question that hung in the air.

Now RJ took a turn at Morrison's hand. "Thanks for everything, man," he said.

After Morrison left, Sagan, Katie and RJ found a place on the floor, Katie resting her head on Sagan's shoulder, careful not to intrude on the site of his injury, and deeply relieved to find that the bleeding was abating. RJ sat on the other side of Katie, staring blankly at a pretty young woman across the way from him, who smiled at him now from the confines of her family. RJ eventually relinquished a small smile before closing his eyes and resting his head against the wall behind him. After a moment, he felt fingers touching his, and looked down to find Katie's hand. It would be a while before he loved a woman again, he told himself, squeezing her hand in his.

He'd been sleeping, or at least he thought he had, when he was awakened by the loud and continuous fire of automatic weapons and someone – he wasn't sure who – saying with a very flat affect, "So much for the cease-fire."

Things went quickly after that, the way the threat of fire will clear a building. And yet there was an almost compulsory orderliness to it, as there was no convenient emergency exit and nowhere to run. Only one recourse was available – to listen carefully to instructions and to follow them with precision.

"Women and children over here," an MP commanded, speaking to the group at large. "Move quickly, please."

"I'm not going without you," Katie told Sagan, panic suddenly setting in.

"Don't be ridiculous," Sagan said, wrapping his arms around her and kissing her cheek. "Kansas really isn't such a bad place, you know," he whispered in her ear.

"I'm not going," she said, suddenly making up her mind.

"We'll go to Colorado, then," he said.

"I'm not going without you," she said, this time with more emphasis.

But Sagan had understood her the first time. Taking off his camera, he handed it to her and said, "Here you go, my darling Katie. Keep this safe for me, will you?"

In the end she acquiesced, not wanting, under the circumstances, to be a problem to anyone. Getting into the line leading from the building to the runway, she waited there to be ushered down the tarmac and into one of the waiting helicopters.

"Now once you get out there, I want you to follow me, get on board, and don't look back. Is that understood?" The MP looked around, seeking comprehension, then added in French, "Tout l'monde a compris?" *Does everyone understand?*

As the MP began to usher the women and children out of the building, Katie found herself moving with the line and, before she knew it, she was on the tarmac and in the heart of intermittent gunfire. She reached for Sagan and RJ for a last goodbye, but they were already well out of reach and, urged on by the MPs, she had no option but to board the waiting helicopter. The roar was so loud that trying to say her goodbyes out loud would have been a futile task. Instead, she located the men she loved at the edge of the building and did her best to convey to them, by way of sheer emotion, all that she felt in her heart.

The helicopter took off quickly, as if urgently called to the heavens by a force greater than its own, and Katie pushed to get a view, taking in the airport as a whole – the fighting factions and, sandwiched in between, the rescue effort still going on. In the bush surrounding the airport, a small segment of Nguesso's supporters broke ground, shooting their way to the tarmac. In the ambush that followed, it was virtually impossible to tell what was what, who was who. The spray of gunfire seemed to hit soldiers and civilians without discrimination. And yet, somehow, in the midst of it all, the efforts to load the shuttles continued.

Frantically, Katie strained to bring Sagan and RJ into view and found them assisting with the evacuation, hurriedly loading the remaining evacuees. Attempting to board the helicopter, a woman was shot in the arm and fell backward, but was quickly lifted in just as the helicopter made a hasty ascent. Those remaining on the ground, Sagan and RJ among them, were left to try to make it on board another helicopter, now wavering between landing and taking off again. Katie's heart was racing now, so fast she thought she would lose consciousness. *Please – please –* she heard the words of her own solemn prayer – *let them make it. Oh, God. Please. Give me the chance to make it up to them.* But she felt her heart quiver and come to a stop when Sagan's run was intercepted by a bullet to the back. Stunned, he stumbled, but somehow gathered his strength and managed, to Katie's intense relief, to keep on going. But the second shot came from the front, felling him instantly, and he collapsed onto his back on the tarmac.

The sky was blue, fading to crystal, as Sagan looked upon it, afraid to let himself close his eyes for fear he might never see her face again. And holding on as long as he could, he scanned the horizon for signs of her helicopter and the fading image of her face at the window – finding instead a bright Paris sky under which the Katie who first stole his heart was talking, her lips moving soundlessly, as if in the frame of a beautiful dream. He strained to hear her and realized that she was reading the words from a tombstone, one moment serious, the other, giddy with laughter. He could hear her every word now and he was all right with it – with the fact that it was his own epitaph that she was reading, and that she found his life both intensely dramatic and devastatingly amusing. But never mind the nuances of his life. All that mattered was that in death he had found her again. For in death, which was (it was as clear to him now as the lopsided grin on her face) a continuum of life – he could see that she loved him truly – as truly as she did that glorious day on the streets of Brazzaville when she put her lips to his – not unthinkingly, as a result of a few clever words that might have accidentally spilled from his lips – but with great certainty, finally and irrevocably awakened to her love for him, and declaring it for all the world to see.

RJ turned, saw that Sagan had fallen, and ran to his side. He fell to his knees, paralyzed for a long moment at the sight of the blood pooling from Sagan's neck. It was obvious that Sagan was dead, the last bullet having pierced the carotid artery. RJ stared incredulously at the blood encroaching on his own being, beginning to stain the knees of his pants. Then, oblivious to the erratic spray of bullets around him and to the blood that would soon cover his own body, RJ lifted Sagan's head and cradled his fallen friend in his arms.

Katie looked down on the scene below with both shock and an almost divine resignation, and as the vision of terror below diminished from her horizon and faded from view, she dropped her head in communion with the Universe that had just taken Sagan's soul.

13

Reunion

JULY 17, 2030

———

 *THE WATER WAS VIRTUALLY STILL,* a shimmering, never-ending blue under the bright Barcelona sun, punctuated only by the white of sailboats in the distance.

Katie took off her shoes to walk barefoot along the Mediterranean shoreline, taking stock of the time that had passed between this moment and the day so many years ago when she had sat crying on the beach for no apparent reason but that the moon was so blue. How old she had felt and how young she had actually been, her hair still dark as midnight, the days and nights ahead too numerous to envision. *How old I must look*, she thought, hating the fact that the flesh had its own timetable that seemed to operate in defiance of the person within. And wondering too if she should have dyed her gray hair for the occasion, or maybe had a little work done on her face. It was so easy these days. But she'd never been inclined to. She was who she was and, anyway, there was nothing to disguise. And nothing to be ashamed of.

Someone had once told her that a life well-lived was like the seasons, each irreplaceable, each inevitably leading to the other, each beautiful in its own right. *Spring was not just the seasonal equivalent of birth, but of re-birth*, Sagan had said. And she had clung to those words, for they had allowed her to believe that she would one day see Sagan's face again.

Apart from an occasional night when sleep hadn't come easily, making random thoughts unavoidable, she hadn't thought about it much in the last dozen years – those first crazy steps into the void of the impossible dream. The resulting nightmare.

But she allowed herself to think of it now – to remember the good with the bad. Her first view of the Congo River from the airplane high above it, RJ's young and exuberant face next to her own. The sunsets and the tragic, unrelenting beauty of the Congo. The encroaching war. The death and dying. Her disbelief at the sight of Sagan approaching on his bicycle – the indescribable joy she had felt when she had finally put her arms around him and known without a doubt that she had always loved him. The instant of his death when she had felt his departure from the world as if his hand had slipped from the grasp of her very own fingers.

When Sagan had died, along with Biyoudi and the millions of other innocents in the long and lingering wars of the Congo (as she would later go to some ends to discover, Biyoudi had not survived his ordeal), she was convinced that her own life had ended – that life had no other plan for her but to bestow its riches upon her for the sheer pleasure of taking them away. The bleak circumstances of the present gave little purpose to her life, but Katie was not by nature a quitter. Still, she seemed to embody George Orwell's words, emblazoned upon her in her youth by Muriel, who could rattle off quotes to defend any argument...

...the ordinary man is passive. Within a narrow circle ... he feels himself master of his fate, but against major events he is as helpless as against the elements ... far from endeavoring to influence the future, he simply lies down and lets things happen to him.

These words came back to her often in the years after Sagan's death. She saw in them the picture, not just of "ordinary men" but, more pointedly, of herself – of the way she had, from the first significant wound on her soul, viewed the world and lived her life.

Yet through some miracle of transference – Sagan's soul to hers? – she had found it again. That will – that faith – the faith that she had renounced at the first sign of life's unpredictability. The inherent love for humanity that she had never been able to manifest until she had lived through and beyond her darkest hour. The realization that it was time to take responsibility, not just for that narrow circle, but for the course of major events which, in the largest sense, were an extension of her very own life. And so it came to be that one night she had laid her head on her pillow, looking forward to the annihilation that sleep would bring, and had awakened the next morning to the sound of birds outside her window and her heart throbbing with renewed purpose. And she had finally arisen from the quicksand of resignation and indifference that had marked the larger part of her existence, to stand on the fertile soil of her own potential.

The irony hadn't been lost on her that, of the three of them, the one to sacrifice his life had not been a true believer. Or if he had believed in anything, it hadn't been the cause so much as the promise of life itself. And yet his death had fueled the Movement. In death, another icon was born.

She made the decision to publish Sagan's letters and photographs, for which she liked to think he had forgiven her. They were, for some, a modest revelation – for others, an awakening. The task of compiling the work had, at first, given her a mission. It had kept her in touch with his soul. In truth, there was an almost spiritual quality to his photographs that she had never recognized before his passing – something about them that made you want to fall on your knees and worship humanity.

She had loved him, and in this she found great consolation. She had loved him and he had felt it and known it and been heightened by it – if only for a few stolen hours. She saw clearly now that she might have turned to nothingness had it not been for the love he had given her those many years – the love he had felt for her despite her own callousness and obliviousness – the passion he had felt for something within her that she herself was too tormented to see. Moreover, she might never have been able to love again had she not been granted a reprieve at the final moment – the chance to say the words he had spent a lifetime longing to hear – and said them while they still counted. They had been heartfelt, and she had whispered them tenderly between kisses in the final hours of their lives together.

And so, when John Morrison made his appearance at her doorstep one fine Colorado fall morning, she was able to let him in – able to listen with compassion and genuine interest as he related the many things that had lain dormant in his heart over the years spent dwelling on his own emptiness. They had found companionship in each other, born of the bonding that is often the result of mutual trauma, of a mutually experienced crisis. She found in him an ally and a friend – like Sagan, a man whose own interests didn't necessarily parallel her own, but who supported her right to be herself.

John had been the perfect partner, though he'd at first been disappointed in her reluctance to have children. How to explain to him that for her, the timeliness of motherhood had simply passed her by, leaving only in its place a stronger affection for the youth of the world and a wish to help raise the next generation of leaders? Maybe he had never understood it. Still, he had wanted her enough to share his days with her. And gradually, his need for children faded and they settled in to enjoy long walks in the mountains and morning coffee together before work – gardening when time permitted, which to him meant cultivating and nurturing, and to her meant sewing seeds with her eyes closed and letting them grow where they fell, untended and unassisted. Sagan had been right when he'd said she should be back in Colorado picking wildflowers. In the end, it was where life found her.

She'd come full circle, she figured. Back to the innocence of youth, the faith of childhood, that innate seed of joy nurtured with every break of day. Back to that place of purity that lies at the core of all people before the muck sets in. In some ways – the most important ones – she was younger now than she was then, despite all physical signs to the contrary. She'd finally been reunited with that child within her – the one that she had so admired in RJ, and so instantly connected to. How good it was to laugh again – to understand that lightness of being is not a slap in the face of the world's suffering, but a gift to the world – that, in fact, it serves to make the world a brighter place. How pleased Sagan would have been to know that she had finally come to this! *I miss that grin*, he had once complained. And, truth be told, so had she.

What is he like? she asked herself, scanning the length of the Mediterranean for signs of the once-young man she hadn't seen in over thirty years. She'd heard lots of talk, rumors, half-truths – scandals even. She'd read about him, seen his picture, watched him age, mature, develop, but only as a public figure – someone removed from the immediacy and relevance of her own life. In all these years – despite moments of thinking of him and always wishing him happiness above all – she hadn't looked into his eyes and known what he was really like, this boy – now a man – who, with little effort beyond showing up at the airport looking for a woman in a yellow dress, once captured her soul and her imagination. A young man who reached into her heart and opened the door for Sagan. In the final analysis, wasn't that what he had done?

She had so often thought of RJ through the years, longed to see him again – been so proud of his accomplishments, the fulfilling of his own impossible dream – longed so much to hear the stories from his own mouth, to see the sparkle in his eye when he got to the punch line. But, at first, the pain of losing Sagan had been too great to share, even with – *especially with* – the only one who could possibly appreciate it. And then, ironically, once the wound had healed, RJ became the only one who could open it again and set it festering.

She'd heard that RJ had made it to Sagan's funeral, and she was glad for that. Sagan would have been pleased. Just as he would have been pleased to know that she had remained at home on the day they had put him in the ground, remembering him from the mountaintop, breathing of his spirit from the fresh mountain air.

And so she consigned RJ to the recesses of her mind, keeping him safe for another day – a day she always believed would come – and, in the meantime, set about her self-appointed tasks, fully determined to live her life according to her own dreams and not the dreams of others. For this had been part of the awakening that was the other side of Sagan's death. No longer would she be the pawn of her father's will, but the servant of her own. No longer would she compare herself to a mother whose own identity was so different from her own. And with that resolve, she had stepped outside the arena of world politics and into the periphery, lending her talents and energy to inspiring the youth of the world to take on their true identities as members of the same global family. This, in the end, would be her mission and her message. That boundaries exist only in the hearts of humankind and that, while a world without boundaries might be the ultimate destination – the proper configuration – it isn't the final frontier.

Love itself is the final frontier.

Samuel's failing, she could define it now, had been his unfortunate inability to get beyond the boundaries in his own heart. That being the case, he was largely ineffective in moving the world in the direction in which his intellect told him it must go. If only he had been able to build within him a heart as vast and as clear as his intellect! What dreams he might have seen come true!

Norwalk, for his part, had died a fairly contented man. Content largely because his dream was not so much to be remembered, or to be right, or even to reach the summit of his own ambitions. His dream had simply been to be true to himself, and this much – even at a plodding pace and exercising judgment that was sometimes lacking – he had been able to do.

To thine own self be true. She repeated the words again, airing them in the cool Barcelona air, knowing that – having sought neither the favor of others, nor fame, nor a place in the annals of history – she had finally managed to live them.

RJ suddenly surfaced from the water, deeply gulping of the air above him. Catching sight of her, he waved and yelled out, "Katie!", then began swimming strongly for shore.

Getting out of the water, his pants dripping wet and clinging stubbornly to his skin, he ignored the stares of his Secret Service agents and colleagues as he took in the sight of the woman who now stood before him, ready to wrap him in the warmth of her sweater.

He went to her and they smiled at each other before falling into each other's arms, a long and purposeful embrace that sought to fill the many years of separation.

"You're still Katie," he finally said, his mind grappling with the wrinkles and gray hair and the many long years that had come between them, but reassured to find the essence of her still vibrant in her dark eyes. *The only constant is change itself,* he was thinking. *And the love in Katie's eyes.*

She touched the scar that ran down his face with her fingertips and took in the full effect of his middle age. Honed. Tempered. Bruised, but resilient. Still beautiful in her eyes.

There's so much to talk about, he was thinking. *So much to tell her. So much I want to know.*

But, in fact, there was too much to talk about, too much life and emotion to catch up on, and only silence was immediately relevant. *Later,* he thought, glad more than anything that it wasn't too late. *Later there'll be time for all of that.* And he slid his arm around her waist, transported to another place and time by the feel of her. A time when he was young and innocent and knew nothing important about living. A time when, in the course of a single week, he learned it all.

Arm in arm, they walked down the beach – slowly – as if careful to leave footsteps on the sands of time – two lovers whose passion for each other had gently evolved into the sweetest, and most enduring of friendships.

Thoughts on a
Federation of the World

It is hard to conceive that a Federation of Planets, which Earthlings like to envision in tales of science fiction, could ever be a reality without the Earth having first transcended its own differences to become a Federation in its own right.

Indeed, such a reality is the vision of many, and began at the end of World War II as the collective dream of those who sought to prevent wide-scale catastrophe from ever happening again by unifying the countries of the world under one governing body. It was from such a dream of peace and global unification that the United Nations was born. However, decades later, despite a claim to many meaningful achievements, especially in the realms of health and human rights, the United Nations – void of any real legislative power – often finds itself in a stalemate of its own bureaucracy, monopolized by the ruling powers of the Security Council, and unempowered to prevent global wars.

Other groups, born around the time of the U.N., have waged a persistent struggle to strengthen the U.N., to amend its charter, and to give it the legislative capacity it requires to be a true peace-keeping force. Still other groups, convinced that the U.N. charter cannot be successfully amended, have worked to create and institute a democratic federal world government under a constitution, aimed at replacing the charter of the United Nations. Among all these groups, as among a growing number of individual citizens, global citizenship is the battle cry and the inevitable framework of the future.

It could be argued that any political structure, no matter how detailed the checks and balances, may still give way to chaos and uncertainty. If that is the case, then the question inevitably becomes, are people ready to conquer their own divisiveness?

As various groups and individuals put their minds together to find a solution to global conflicts and the growing environmental crises that plague our planet, the way made easier by the Internet and the many advancements in communication technologies, a Federation of Earth, legislatively empowered and with pacifism and compassion at its core, may well prove to be the political, environmental, and economic salvation of the planet.

But as Katie Cagle finally came to realize after enduring the gamut of life's tribulations, a world without boundaries might be the ultimate destination – indeed, the proper configuration – but the final frontier is one that exists at the heart of every human being. Ultimately, it is the forging of this frontier which will give rise to an enlightened political structure, illuminating the world just as surely and as gracefully as the moon coming over the mountain.